Charles Gibbon

In Love and War

A romance. Vol.1

Charles Gibbon

In Love and War
A romance. Vol. 1

ISBN/EAN: 9783337065751

Printed in Europe, USA, Canada, Australia, Japan

Cover: Foto ©Andreas Hilbeck / pixelio.de

More available books at **www.hansebooks.com**

IN LOVE AND WAR.

A Romance.

BY

CHARLES GIBBON,

AUTHOR OF "IN HONOUR BOUND," "ROBIN GRAY,"
"WHAT WILL THE WORLD SAY?" "FOR LACK OF GOLD," ETC.

IN THREE VOLUMES.

VOL. I.

LONDON:

RICHARD BENTLEY AND SON,

NEW BURLINGTON STREET.

1877.

CONTENTS OF VOL. I.

—◦◦◦—

IN LOVE AND WAR.

CHAPTER I.

THE HOT TROD.

"He's ta'en her by the milk-white hand,
    And by the grass-green sleeve.
He's mounted her high behind himsel',
    At her kinsmen spear'd na leave."

Katherine Janfarie.

"BRING out the hounds, Nicol," shouted Sir Hugh Janfarie, the Knight of Johnstone Tower, to his second son; and then to one of his men: "You fetch me a burning sod. It shall be a Hot Trod, and by the Sacred

1

Mother a hotter trod than has been known on the Border this while."

He mounted his horse and took his place at the head of his men; a leash of hounds was brought from the kennel, and the party started at a round pace.

Nicol rode in advance, carrying a burning turf on the point of a spear, to denote to all men that they had declared hue and cry against a marauder, and that they were in hot pursuit. The fiery symbol of their purpose, according to the law of the Marches, protected them from interruption so long as they molested none save the enemy they pursued. The same law doomed to death any who might attempt to bar the way of those who, with proper reason, were following the track of an offender.

Katherine Janfarie, Sir Hugh's only daughter, and Sir Bertrand Gordon, the Laird of Lamington, were the offenders, and the objects of this fierce pursuit.

Sir Hugh had that day forced his daughter into marriage with Sir Robert Cochrane, the chief favourite of the king, James III.; Katherine had wept, implored, defied—refused even in presence of the priest to accept the man chosen by her parents as her husband—but all without avail. The ceremony proceeded, and she was declared to be duly wedded to Cochrane. Kinsmen and retainers were hospitably entertained; bonfires were prepared, and sports went forward just as if it had been one of the happiest matches ever known on the Border.

A marauding expedition of Sir Hugh and his two sons—Richard, the master of Johnstone, and Nicol—had drawn down upon them the wrath of the Duke of Albany, then Lord Warden of the Marches. He had seized the greater part of their holdings, threatened to lay waste their home, and to drive them from the land, root and branch. As Albany was then in high favour with the English Court, the Janfaries could not hope for any succour from that quarter. Under ordinary circumstances they might have calculated upon such succour. Their sole hope of rescue centred in King James, and he could only be reached successfully through his favourite, Cochrane. Him Sir Hugh sought, knowing that he had no kindly regard for the king's brother, Albany; and whatever might have been the nature of their interview, the result was that Cochrane pledged himself to restore the lands of Sir Hugh, and to protect him from Albany's vengeance. He fulfilled his pledge to the letter.

That was the service he had rendered the family, and the price was the hand of Katherine Janfarie.

To those who knew Cochrane, the price seemed a poor one for so much service; but none doubted that he had good reasons for making such a bargain, and for insisting upon its fulfilment in despite of the objections the lady raised. He had reasons, and potent ones. His influence over the king seemed to increase daily; but, in proportion, the hate with which he was regarded by the noblemen whose places he usurped at Court, and by the people whose rights he trampled upon, also increased. On this account he sought alliance with some family, at whose command a sufficiently considerable force could be brought into the field to serve in a degree as a protection against his enemies. There were other reasons for his present course, but they were known only to himself; and he kept his own counsel.

The rejoicings were at their height,

when Sir Bertrand Gordon made his way
secretly into the tower. The unhappy
bride, who, with despairing hope, had
looked for his coming, met her lover.
They passed unseen to the court; he lifted
her up beside him on his horse, Falcon,
and before a hand could be raised to
stay them, they were through the gateway
and beyond reach.

Then ensued wild confusion, exclama-
tions of rage, and threats of vengeance.
The bridegroom and the elder brother
Richard were the first mounted and in
pursuit. But it was not long before Sir
Hugh had raised the symbol of the hot-
trod, and, with fifty picked men, his
kinsmen, Musgrave and Fenwick, by his
side, and sure-scented hounds to guide
them, followed in the track of the lovers.

The darkening gloaming favoured the
fugitives as they were borne along by the

swift-footed horse. Falcon proved himself worthy of his name, and every encouraging sound of his master's voice seemed to inspire him with new strength; he seemed to have almost a human sense of the perilous venture in which he played so prominent a part.

The horse dashed through the shadows which seemed like giant forms reaching towards him to bar the way, and which were baffled by his speed. Now the black irregular line of the Annan water came in view; and as Falcon approached the ford in the direction of which he had been guided, it became evident that his strength was failing. He had been ridden far and fast that day to reach Johnstone Tower, and now the unusual strain that had been put upon his power began to tell.

This Lamington would fain have concealed from his companion, but she was

quick to observe how much more frequently he required to speak, urging the
jaded animal forward. When they had
forded the Annan, voice and spur prompted
Falcon into a gallop, but the effort he
made was apparent. His pace was slower,
he snorted heavily at every bound, and
those grim shadows of surrounding objects
seemed to stoop closer and longer over him.

"If he should fail us now," she said,
raising her pale face, "they will overtake
us and they will kill you."

"Have no fear. Falcon will hold out
until we reach Dumfries, and there I hope
to find a friend waiting with fresh horses
to carry us in safety to our journey's end."

"Safety," she echoed, doubtingly. "Ah,
Bertrand, where in all Scotland shall we
find that now? We have made relentless
enemies of my father and my brothers, and
there is no resting-place to which they will
not follow us."

"I do not fear that, either; for, give me only a few days, and I will satisfy them that I have rescued you from the hands of a villain—one so foul at heart that, knowing him, no man would stir a step in his cause."

"You will never satisfy them of that."

"Well, if the worst happen, we can defend ourselves."

She started suddenly, straining her eyes into the gloom behind.

"Did you hear?" she cried.

"I heard nothing but the wind."

"It was like the baying of a hound."

"That might have been, and yet give us no cause for trouble. But it is your fancy that plays tricks with you. Come, Falcon, lad, complete the work you have begun so well. On, lad, on; there is only a little space to cover now."

Katherine was silenced, but not satisfied.

The horse responded to the new command with a mighty effort; but his speed soon relaxed again, to be again quickened by voice and spur.

The constant effort to sustain the horse became almost as fatiguing to the rider as the exertion it produced was to the animal. A fair speed, however, was maintained; and at length, as they neared Dumfries, the towers of Grey Friars and St. Michael loomed up darkly against the lowering sky.

Then Bertrand permitted Falcon to slacken pace, and enter the town at a jaded walk. The douce burgesses, who in those days observed the simple rule of bedding soon after sunset and rising with the lark, had, for the most part, retired to rest, and were undisturbed by the ring of the horse's slow steps. There were, however, gleams of light in a few windows where a late feast or sickness caused some of the folk to make a breach in the rule. A pale sickly light illumed several of the windows of the monastery of Grey Friars—in the chapel of which Comyn was slain by Bruce and his followers. The black outline of the ancient castle of the Maxwells rose protectingly above the sleeping town, and the lights gleaming through the portholes of the guard house indicated that watch and ward were observed.

The better to avoid the curious gaze of any loiterer, Lamington passed down by the warder's dyke towards the Nith. On reaching the margin of the broad waste called the Sands, which were at high tide covered with water, and at the ebb left bare and yellow, he turned in the direction of the bridge of Devorgilla.

Almost opposite to the bridge, and distant from it not more than two hundred

yards, was a square, white house, of two
storeys in height, and roofed with thick,
brown thatch. It had a squat, comfortable
look in daylight, and stood in the midst
of a cluster of small houses. It had three
entrance doors, one giving to the High
Street, the second, an equally important
one, giving to the bridge; and the third,
at the side, was used only for communi-
cation with the stables. This was the
principal hostelry of the town, and was
called the Royal Hunt, on account of its
having been the resting-place of the king's
party on the way to the royal forest of
Kells. Matthew Hislop was the vintner,
and he was soon brought to the door by
the loud summons of Lamington, although
the house had been closed for the night.

The vintner was a stout fellow of middle
age, who before he had settled down to
his present occupation had proved the

strength of his limbs in many a Border wrestling bout, and in not a few fights of a more questionable character.

He stared in some astonishment at the appearance of the cavalier and the lady with one horse. The worn-out appearance of the latter, its hide covered with foam and bespattered with mud, were suggestive of a ride that had not been altogether one of pleasure. Whatever suspicions might have been aroused in his mind, he was not permitted to express them, even if he had intended to do so.

Bertrand hastily inquired if he had any guest waiting for a friend.

"Was there any sign?" queried the vintner, cautiously.

"Yes, the man's belt is buckled with a boar's head such as this."

Opening his cloak the knight displayed the silver buckle of his own sword belt which was formed like a boar's head.

"It's the Gordon," muttered Hislop, recognizing the badge of the family; "na, the chiel ye want is no here."

Lamington gave vent to an exclamation of disappointment, and then, hastily: "Show me your best chamber, and get the horse taken to the stable. There are twenty crowns for you if you serve me faithfully to-night."

This promise infused sudden alacrity into the movements of the host; and whilst he conducted his guests to his principal chamber upstairs, an ostler took the horse round to the stable.

The vintner, promptly obeying the orders he had received, spread the table with the best repast his larder could supply at the moment; and whilst he was thus occupied, Lamington questioned him as to the possibility of obtaining a couple of good horses.

"There's no a brute in the stable that could travel five miles the night," was the disappointing answer.

"Can you not borrow from some of your neighbours?"

"No—at any rate, I cannot think o' ane that could oblige ye, for the morn's fair day at Lockerbie, and a' the horse and cattle that's worth a straw are awa' there."

"We must wait, then, for Will's arrival, or we must start again after Falcon has had a rest," was the disagreeable conclusion which the knight was compelled to accept.

Hislop was retiring, when he was stayed by Lamington touching his arm.

"See you, master vintner, should ill luck bring you other guests to-night, than the man we are looking for, give us timely warning; and take heed that they know nothing of our presence here. Be faithful, and the twenty crowns may be doubled."

"I ken what's what," nodded the vintner discreetly, "and I gie you my word that nae harm shall come to ye or the bonnie lady in my house."

"Enough, see you to the comfort of my horse; we may have to depend on his speed again."

The door closed upon Hislop, and Gordon turned to the lady.

CHAPTER II.

FORESHADOWS.

"Say, should we scorn joy's transient beams
Because to-morrow storms may lour?"

Glenfinlas.

THE room was long and narrow, with two windows opening to the high street. It was lit by a cresset hanging from the low roof by an iron chain. The light scattered the darkness from the centre of the chamber, but permitted it to form in dark shadows in the corners, and to give the larger pieces of the massive furniture a gloomy aspect. The feeble light, the big shadows, and the quietude of the night, rendered the appearance of the apartment cold and dismal.

Lamington was surprised to see Katherine with her head bowed on the table and her hands clasped as if she were in pain. Anxiously he raised her head and gazed in her eyes, which were full of tears.

" Katherine, do you fear our fate so much that all your courage has forsaken you ? "

She answered him low and tremulously.

" No, Bertrand ; I do not fear our fate, whatever that may be ; but I fear the course which has led us to it."

" You mean that you are calmer now, and that you regret the sacrifice you have made for my sake ? "

" Not that ; I regret nothing that is done for your sake, and had you come to me before they had forced me to the altar I would have been happy now, and could have met the dangers that arise at every step with a firm heart."

" Why then be sad ? "

She glanced round the room shudderingly.

" They told me I was his wife—and Heaven itself frowns upon the woman who breaks the sacred tie of wedlock. He has the right to claim me; to drag me from you, and the mighty voice of the Church supports his claim. Whilst he lives I can never call you husband."

" You made no vow," he cried earnestly; " you were forced to the altar; the coward priest, who was unworthy of his high office, performed the ceremony in terror of his own wretched life; and the Church will refuse to acknowledge such a mockery of its most holy rites."

" If that be so, a weary burden is lifted from my heart."

" It is so, as you shall find before many hours are past. I carry you now to the Abbot Panther, and he shall protect you until the Pope himself shall have annulled every claim that Cochrane might have upon you. A few weeks will suffice to obtain your release, and until then regard me as your friend—your brother who devotes his life to your happiness."

" You give me new strength, and henceforth you shall find me as fearless and unfaltering as yourself."

He pressed her hand respectfully to his lips.

" That is Katherine Janfarie who is speaking now, and not the timid maiden who trembles at the shadows of her own fancy. Remember, there must be no more doubts—no more lingering looks cast backward, or I shall doubt your love."

She clasped his arms spasmodically.

"You must never doubt that," she cried, "for it would kill me. I have forsaken all the world for you. I have staked even the good name, which is my highest treasure; and if you doubt me after that, there is nothing more to live for."

"I will never doubt," he said, in a low, passionate tone, "until you yourself shall say you wish you had not loved me."

"When you prove false, my misery may wring from me such a cry as that, but no other power can move me to it."

"And when I do prove false you shall have the right to spurn me."

Their eyes were bright with confidence, undimmed by any speck of dread of the possible terrors the future might have in store.

"Come," he said presently, with a happy laugh, "I see the tears are gone from your eyes, which tell me that all doubt

has vanished from your mind. Be ever so
—look always thus, and you will find me
always at your feet—your slave. Ay, by
my faith, as much your slave when wedded
years have passed, with all their petty
bickerings, as now, when we are looking
to the future through the bright halo of
hopeful love."

"That is a pledge," she said, affected by
his good humour, and the grave trouble of
her visage disappeared in a smile.

"A pledge it is, and you shall christen
it with me in this wine. Come, we will be
merry while we have this moment to rest,
and I will describe our course to you."

He spoke with the ease of one uncon-
scious of danger, and with the gaiety of
one who is perfectly happy. This naturally
influenced her, and before many minutes
had passed she was almost as merry as if
there were no peril near.

" First, I have to place you under the safe keeping of Abbot Panther," he proceeded gaily; " he is one who fears neither king nor baron. He has the power, and I believe he has the will to serve me. I journeyed with him from France, where he is Abbot of Poitou; and I have a tryste with him at Kells. He is 'the Pope's Legate, and once under his protection the king himself will hesitate to force your inclination, even in behoof of his favourite, Cochrane."

" But the king will visit his displeasure with him on you."

" Most like he will; but there is a way by which I hope to overcome it. His brothers, Albany and Mar, hold me in some esteem—I dare swear esteem as high as their dislike for Cochrane is deep. With their aid I hope to satisfy our royal master that in this matter I have done nothing save that which an honourable gentleman must have done ; and that in other matters I have served him best when he condemned me most—in proving the falseness of the knave who is now chief in his counsels."

"Take heed, Bertrand, take heed ; it is a dangerous path you seek to tread."

"The more honour in the victory."

"Ay, but in this the odds are too much against you. If it were in the field of battle that you had to prove yourself, I would buckle on your sword, and watch with proud eyes your steps to victory—or death" (trembling a little at that word). "I have no fear when the foeman stands declared before you in the light of day. Then I would pray the Sacred Mother to watch over you, and could wait the issue calmly. But in this course you mark out, you have to deal with wolves and foxes in the dark, scarce knowing who is your friend and who your enemy. It is not the sword of a gentleman that can protect you; you must wield the weapons of the knaves you fight against; cunning must be your brand, and artifice your shield."

" Be it so; at least I shall use them honestly, and for a worthy purpose."

" Why use them at all ? "

" Because there is no other way to justice."

" Then why seek such justice ? Why not be content in having that man's claim to me annulled, and in taking me to your home ? We can be very happy there, making a world of our own, whilst all the storms and miseries of ambition and intrigue pass by us unheeded."

His brow became clouded, and his hands clenched. Then sadly :

" My home, Katherine—have you forgotten ?—my home is where my sword or

wit may cleave a way for me. The old
tower stands yonder by the eerie Loch of
Var, and it will give us shelter from the
wind and rain when the need comes. But
it can give us no protection from the spite
of men. It is garrisoned by two old ser-
vitors who have been faithful to our house
in its misfortune as in its triumph, and
their son—the fellow who should have met
us here. They are strong enough to hold
it, for it owns nothing that is worth any
man's lifting. The lands around it, which
once gave its owners the right to stand
abreast with the foremost of the country,
are not ours now, but the king's, since my
father was falsely charged with aiding
Douglas in slaying Maclellan of Bombie.
That sentence must be revoked; those
lands must be restored to me before I cease
to war with whatever weapons my need
may demand."

Katherine's reply was interrupted by the baying of a hound, and the clatter of horses' hoofs rising above the whistling of the wind.

Bertrand sprang to the casement, and, slightly parting the hangings, peered forth. He saw two horsemen disappearing in the direction of the stable.

"If I am not happily mistaken," he whispered hurriedly, "it is your brother and Cochrane who have made upon us. We must try Falcon again."

Katherine leaped to her feet, and drew close over her head the cloak her lover had placed round her. She had become pale at the announcement of the pursuers' arrival, but she was firm and decisive in her movements.

The door suddenly opened, and Hislop entered with much confusion in his manner.

"Your horse is dead, sir," he said, under

his breath, and closing the door after him.

"Dead!" ejaculated the fugitives together.

"Ay, dead, sir, and a bonnie beast he was tae; but ye hae ridden him owre sair. He wad neither take bite nor sup when we got him into the stable; he just drappit doon pechan' his life out, and he died just as I was wetting his mou' wi' some o' the best Malmsey."

"Why did you not call me sooner?" said Bertrand, angrily.

"I didna want to disturb ye, sir; and maybe it was as weel, for there are twa gentlemen hae just ridden into the yard, and the youngest o' them saw your horse, and said he would swear it was Lamington's. By that he ken'd that ye and the lady were in the house, and they're seeking ye up and down."

"Where are they?"

"One o' them's keeping guard in the lobby, and the ither's turning every room he comes tae tapsalteerie. But ye just unlock yon door ahint ye wi' the key ye see hanging on it, and it opens on a stair that'll tak' ye doon tae the kitchen, and the guidwife will try to slip ye oot, while I try tae get that chiel tae quit the lobby."

"Where are their horses?"

"In the stable-yard."

Bertrand seized the key from the nail on which it hung, and opened the narrow door which gave to the private staircase.

Katherine uttered an exclamation of amaze, and Bertrand drew back a pace, for the moment the door was opened they were confronted by Sir Robert Cochrane!

Searching the house, Cochrane had discovered the entrance to the staircase in the kitchen, and followed it with this result.

CHAPTER III.

THE BROKEN SWORD.

"But hark, what means yon faint halloo?
The chase is up—but they shall know
The stag at bay's a dangerous foe."

SCOTT.

THERE was a peculiarly cold smile on Cochrane's sallow visage, and a gratified glitter in his eyes, as he noted the effect his unexpected appearance created. He spoke with a tone of satiric civility, affecting to treat the whole transaction as only a jest which had been carried a little too far.

"You have afforded us excellent sport,

Master Gordon," he said, showing a row
of white teeth, through which the words
passed hissingly, "and you, too, mistress, we have to thank you for this
merry game of hide-and-seek ; but I am
afraid, the hiders being found, the game
must end."

"Stand aside, sir," cried Lamington,
fiercely ; " we are in no mood for jests, and
least of all from you."

Cochrane did not move, and he addressed
himself directly to Katherine.

"Madam, as your husband, and as one
holding some position that may not be
lightly tarnished, I must beg you to accompany me straight to your home. We will
forget this little excursion you have made,
somewhat against my will, and we will try
to keep all knowledge of it from those who
might judge it more harshly than I wish
to do."

Her face crimsoned, and an angry light shone in her eyes. Contempt, scorn, and defiance were in her look as she answered him:

" The title you claim was obtained by force. No word or look of mine gave assent to the bond which you hold over me. Foully and cruelly it was thrust upon me, and the dear Virgin be my witness now that I renounce it utterly—I spurn it from me, and no power on earth shall ever make me yield to it."

The cold smile—cruel and satanic almost in its expression—became more marked on Cochrane's face.

" You are my wife, madam, despite your brave renunciation of my title to call you so. But, however strong you may feel in your determination now, I doubt not that in time you will learn wisdom and forswear this girlish passion—ay, and regret it too."

He spoke with irritating coolness and confidence.

She would have answered again, but Gordon prevented her.

"Hush, Katherine! have no more words with him. This fellow understands no argument of goodness or justice; but there is one law he understands—that of necessity, and we must put him to it."

Whilst he had been speaking, Cochrane, although watching him closely, had bent his head as if listening for the sound of some one coming, and he was apparently satisfied with the result.

"You are a valiant gentleman, Master Gordon," he said, sneeringly; "you have proved yourself worthy of the name you bear, and I own that I would rather have called you friend than foe. Since that may not be, I salute you with all due respect as a worthy enemy in the field or in the

3

council chamber. But, as a gentleman, I think you can scarcely deny my right to remove that lady."

Gordon with difficulty restrained himself during the delivery of these cynical remarks, and he answered impatiently:

" Fine words, sir, will not prove your right ; but you have a sword, and it may. On guard."

Giving Cochrane no more time than to place himself in a position of defence, Gordon assailed him with rapid and vigorous passes which only an experienced swordsman could have parried Cochrane seemed to be more intent at first upon discovering the peculiar method of his opponent's play, than upon giving thrust for thrust. For the moment his coolness and his purely defensive action seemed to give him the advantage. But at the instant when he seemed to have discovered the trick of his antagonist's fence, and was about to avail himself of that knowledge in a deadly lounge, Lamington, by a dexterous swirl of his sword, wrenched Cochrane's out of his hand.

Cochrane stood astounded, and at the mercy of his enemy. The sword point was at his breast, when Katherine threw herself upon her lover's arm.

"Not yet, Bertrand," she cried, "not in my sight. Let him live until the world knows his baseness, and some vulgar hand strikes him to the earth."

Gordon sheathed his weapon, and picked up from the floor that of Cochrane.

"If you were capable of gratitude," he said, sternly, "I would bid you be grateful to this lady for your wretched life. As it is, I am content to obey her wish, unworthy as you are of one merciful thought. But thus I show my scorn of your knighthood."

So saying, he broke the sword across his knee, and flung the pieces at the man's feet.

"You have given me a lesson," said the defeated man, or rather hissed, for his teeth were clenched and more displayed than usual, "and I thank you. I will not forget it. I know your trick, and it will not serve you a second time."

"By St. Michael, the second time will ring the death-knell of one of us. Take up your sword, broken though it be; it is a worthier weapon than you have any right to wear. Now, stand aside."

Gripping him by the arm, he whirled him across the floor. At the same time Hislop, who had contrived to hide himself from Cochrane's view by stooping behind one of the chairs in the obscurity of the corner, darted forward and extinguished the cresset throwing the chamber into complete darkness.

Gordon's hand was fortunately on the door, and he passed through, drawing Katherine after him. He took the precaution to remove the key from the inside, and so locked the door when he got out, making their outwitted enemy a prisoner.

They descended a dark narrow flight of stairs, and suddenly found themselves in the kitchen of the hostelry, which was occupied only by Dame Hislop, and a man who was stretched on a wooden settle, fast asleep and snoring loudly.

The dame was a broad-shouldered, big-boned woman, with rather harsh features, but with good-humoured eyes that softened them even to a kindly look.

"Oh, sirs," she exclaimed, in an under-tone, "but this is the maist awsome night that ever was. Dinna ye hear the racket that's in the toon and gathering about our house, as if the deil himsel' had ta'en quarters in it, and the folk were gaun to drive him out wi' flaming swords and a smell o' his ain brimstone? We'll hae the big drum beating in a minute, and the whale toon will be skelpin' about in its sark."

These observations were made rather to herself than to her guests, whose presence she seemed scarcely to observe until she had finished. Her words drew the attention of Katherine and Lamington to the disturbance without, which in the excitement of the encounter with Cochrane they had not observed sooner.

There was a loud confusion of voices, the baying of hounds, the trampling of horses' hoofs, and the general din made by an excited crowd. Presently to this was added the loud beating of a drum, answered by shouts and watch-cries from various points of the town.

Hislop burst into the kitchen.

"It's a Hot Trod that's after ye," he gasped, "and the toon's rising. Do ye no hear the drum beating as though a' the deils in the Border were making an assault? Saints save us, if it's ken'd that I hae been hiding ye, it's as muckle as my life's worth."

"Can we not pass forth?" said Gordon. "We will be safer in the midst of the crowd than here."

"Ods my life, man, ye canna gang out; the house is surrounded wi' Border prickers. Gie them some duds, guid wife, to cast ower their ain, whilst I try and put the folk aff the scent."

He rushed out, and as he did so there was a tramp of heavy footsteps in the passage.

CHAPTER IV.

THE DISGUISE.

"There were four and twenty bonnie boys
    A' clad in Johnstone grey;
They said they would take the bride again
    By the strong hand if they may.

"Some o' them were right willing men,
    But they were na willing a';
And four and twenty Leader lads
    Bid them mount and ride awa'."

Katherine Janfarie.

THE din without grew louder as the startled burgesses, half-dressed, and armed with the first weapons that had offered to their hands, hastened to the scene of the alarm. Here the burning peat which Nicol Janfarie held aloft on his spear declared the purpose of the untimely disturbance; and every good man and true was thereby bound to render what assistance might be in his power to seize the fugitives.

Many of the townsfolk were the more readily disposed to comply with the rule out of spite for the alarm they had undergone, and for the disagreeable interruption of their slumbers. Some there were, however, who, on learning the nature of the "cattle" which had been lifted, were rather inclined to enter upon the search as a sport than with any serious desire to arrest the defaulters. These were the younger men, whose sympathies were naturally on the side of the lovers; whilst the former were the elders, who had more regard for their own comfort than for Cupid's perplexities, and who had daughters of their own to protect against moonlight lovers.

The babble and turmoil swelled and lingered in the neighbourhood of the Royal Hunt, and at the moment when Hislop had been in the kitchen announcing the rising of the town and the discovery of the retreat of the Laird of Lamington and his lady by Sir Hugh Janfarie and his followers, an entrance to the house had been forced.

Hislop immediately placed himself at the command of the Borderers, with such an appearance of frankness that no suspicion was aroused of the deception he was practising.

"Come this gate, gentlemen," he said, proceeding up the stair; "I think the folk ye're seeking are up here."

He led them through every room, leaving the one in which Cochrane was confined to the last. He submitted to many threats and curses as chamber after chamber failed to reward the pursuers with the slightest clue to the whereabouts of their prey.

At last they discovered Cochrane, whose attempts to make himself heard by his friends had been drowned in the wild tumult of voices, the trampling of feet, and the clatter of arms within and without the house.

Cochrane's explanation was briefly given, and by his direction the private door was forced. Then he, with Sir Hugh and several men, rushed down to the kitchen, whilst Richard and the rest of the party descended by the ordinary passage to prevent the egress of their victims, whom they now felt assured were run to earth.

When the Borderers burst into the kitchen by both entrances almost simultaneously, the guidwife raised a skirl of alarm, and seized a broomstick, as if to defend herself.

" Saunts preserve a' body!" she cried, with more of a termagant's rage in her manner than of a woman's fear, " what are ye folk doin' rampaging about like a wheen stots afore a riever? Are ye gaun to ding the biggin' about our lugs? or are ye gaun to harry the hostel that's under the king's ain favour, forbye that o' the Grey Friars and the lord o' the castle? What do ye mean, ye ill-faured loons, breaking into a decent man's house this gate?"

The excited gentlemen and as many of their followers as had been able to crowd into the apartment were brought to a standstill. Cochrane, Sir Hugh, and Richard glared round the place with wrathful chagrin.

The persons they sought were not there.

Besides the hostess they saw another woman and two men. The woman was young, and was standing by the dresser, on which she had been baking cakes, when the sudden invasion of the place interrupted and frightened her. She wore a brown petticoat, and a loose yellow short-gown or body, the sleeves of which were tucked above her elbows, and her arms were white with barley meal. On her head she wore a " mutch "—a big frilled cap—and what hair was visible had been touzled and so whitened with meal that it would have defied the keenest eyes to have detected its colour by the feeble aid the lamp afforded. One of her eyes appeared to have received some injury, and a red kerchief was tied across it, to the destruction of whatever comeliness her face possessed.

Scared by the uproar, she stood in a shrinking posture by the dresser, holding up the yellow crock in which she had been mixing the meal, as if ready to heave it at the first who molested her. This little trick at the same time served to shadow her features, and to render it almost impossible for any of the men to obtain a clear view of her face, whilst it imparted a certain gaukiness to her figure which none of them could have associated with Katherine Janfarie.

A big clumsy fellow, in the coarse garb of a common hind, was stretched on the wooden settle, and he only noticed the intrusion by a drowsy growl of discontent, as he turned his face to the wall to sleep again.

The other man was standing by the huge fireplace with a mug of ale raised to his mouth, where it had apparently been arrested by his surprise and curiosity at the Borderers' furious entry.

He stood directly under the lamp, and as he wore one of the broad-crowned bonnets used by farmers, the shadow it cast over his face in the position he occupied, rendered his features barely visible. He had the appearance of a drover, and he seemed to have either just arrived from a journey or to have been about to start on one. A large grey plaid covered his shoulders and body, and the ends of it almost touched the top of his high jack-boots. In one hand he grasped a heavy-headed whip, and in the other the mug of ale was poised.

He had a rough rustic bearing, through which it would have been difficult to identify the cavalier who had studied gallantry at the Court of France.

It was rendered unnecessary, and indeed impossible for the drover or the one-eyed cakemaker to speak, by the running fire of complaint and indignation which the hostess kept up with unabated vigour of lungs and words.

"Peace, woman," commanded Sir Hugh, when he had gazed round without observing anything suspicious—"peace, woman, and acquaint us where you have hidden the guests who were with you but now."

"Me hidden them!" exclaimed the hostess, with renewed energy. "My certes, and what would I do that for? I hae enough ado to wait on them without playing bairn's pranks with them."

"Cease your railing, Jezebel, and answer me——"

The hostess interrupted him with a shriek of rage, and flourished her broomstick with so much effect that she cleared a space around her.

"Jessie bell or Jessie pat yersel'—I'm nane," she vociferated. "And I'll no be put upon in my ain house."

The drover gave vent to a guttural "Haw, haw," as if the scene amused him.

Cochrane stepped up to the woman and spoke civilly.

"You mistake, dame; no offence to you was intended; and pray you answer us without fear and without waste of time— where have the lady and the fellow who was with her upstairs gone? If they are in the house, declare it at once; for we will find them, and your attempt to shield them will not be to your benefit or theirs."

"Ye're a civil spoken gentleman; but I ken nought o' the folk, sae ye may keep your civility for some ither body."

"You must know something of them; so be wise and answer."

"I'll answer that," broke in the drover, speaking hoarsely, and as if he had something in his mouth.

"You!" said Cochrane, eyeing him keenly.

The man stood the inspection unmoved.

But the girl at the dresser seemed to be strangely affected by his sudden speech, and also by the fact that Richard Janfarie was staring at her with puzzled looks. The yellow crock dropped from her hands to the floor, and she stooped down to pick up the fragments.

Dame Hislop, observing Janfarie's curious glances, rushed towards the lass, and with affected spleen, assailing her, contrived to take a position which concealed her from the man's view.

" Ye stupid, handless taupie, ye'll hae a' the dishes in the house broken in nae time," she cried, giving the lass a slap on the shoulder that made her stagger.

She continued to abuse her and to keep beside her, and the anger was so well feigned, that it lulled the rising suspicions which had come so near enabling Richard to penetrate the disguise.

"Aye, me," proceeded the drover, hoarsely, "if ye mean the lady and gentleman wha came out o' that door there—I can tell ye what gate they hae taen, for it was me direckit them."

"Say it, fellow," ejaculated Sir Hugh, impatiently; "where are they hidden?"

"They are nae mair hid than I am, sae far as I ken. The gentleman said he wanted horses, and I told him to gang up the back wynd to the monastery, whare they wad maybe get them."

"Are you sure of that?"

"I think sae; but as they can scarcely hae got to the gate yet, ye had better gang after them and see."

Sir Hugh turned to his son and directed him to have every door and window of the house guarded, so that no one might leave during his absence.

Cochrane was less satisfied than his

friend with the drover's voluntary information.

"Show me your hand," he said, seizing the man's arm; "it seems to me little used to rough work such as your garb would betoken you as accustomed to."

"Od maister, do ye think that? Now, that's just what my friends say; but it has got a hard grip, saft as it looks."

And with that he grasped Cochrane's wrist with a force that would have made an ordinary man wince. When the drover removed his hand it left a blue ring round the wrist.

The consequence of this slight incident might have been fatal to the fugitives, had there not been at the moment a cry raised outside which seemed to shape itself into the words—

"They are found! they are found!"

Sir Hugh rushed out to discover the

cause of the new commotion, and if necessary to proceed to the monastery. He
was followed by Richard and the men ; but
Cochrane remained.

"You have a stout gripe," he said,
carelessly, and still watching the man
narrowly.

"I said that."

"And your boast was truer than boasts
generally are. What is your name ?"

The abrupt question was made with a
purpose. A moment's hesitation would
have betrayed the real character of the
drover, which his hand had made Cochrane suspect. But he responded on the
instant.

"Will Craig I'm called, and whiles
Muckle Will."

"I will remember the name. Do you
know whom we are seeking ?" (Another
trial question, abrupt as before.)

" Ye didna say." (Indifferently, and placing the ale mug to his lips.)

" The man we are seeking is called Gordon of Lamington."

The drover finished his draught, and then, wiping his lips :

" Aye, I think I hae heard the name afore."

" Wha said Lamington ? " was the unexpected inquiry, made in a deep bass.

Cochrane wheeled about, and looked at the man who had been sleeping on the settle, and who was now sitting up rubbing his eyes with the sleeve of his jerkin in a slow stupid way. Cochrane's movement prevented him observing the sudden start of the drover as he observed the face of the lout.

" I spoke of Lamington," said Cochrane. " Have you seen him ? "

The man ceased rubbing his eyes and

looked up at the speaker with an expression
of drowsy curiosity.

"I dinna ken you, onyway," he answered
in his heavy voice, "and it's nae business
o' yours wha I hae seen."

With that he opened a capacious mouth
in a long yawn, and when his jaws were
stretched to the utmost his eyes lighted on
the drover. His mouth closed with a loud
snap, and he jumped up, crying:

"The maister himsel'."

The drover thrust him angrily back as
the clown sprang to him with an expression
of joyous recognition on his broad simple
visage.

"Ye hae had ower muckle ale, Will,"
said the drover, addressing the man by the
name he had given as his own. "Did ye
no hear the gentleman saying that here's a
brave company of Borderers wha hae raised
the Hot Trod against ane Lamington?"

The heavy jaw of the sleepy-headed fellow dropped, and he looked with some bewilderment from the drover to Cochrane. Slowly he seemed to comprehend something, and still in a drowsy way he began to move towards the door. He passed out.

Cochrane, whose conduct in the interview with the drover was that of one who suspects, and who is conscious that his suspicions are baffled at every turn, appeared to hesitate for an instant. Then he followed the man.

"The blundering fool!" muttered the drover, without any of the hoarseness which had disguised his voice; "the addle-pated knave! I doubt not he has been sleeping there since our arrival, and he shows himself now when escape must be made through a thousand dangers. Katherine!"

The lass who had broken the crock, and

who during the foregoing scene had busied herself in conjunction with the hostess in the baking, turned to him—

"Speak low," she said warningly; "I have heard everything. I fear he suspects you, and that man who was sleeping here seemed to recognize you."

"He is my follower, Will Craig—the knave whom I expected to find here with horses."

"Cochrane has followed him," was her distressed cry. "He will cajole the secret from him."

"Not with his life. The rascal has only one faculty, but that one is fidelity to me. Dolt as he is in other respects, no torture could force from him a word that might injure me. You might have marked that I gave him warning of our peril the instant I recognized him, and he seemed to understand."

"But if he be so dull of wit, he may forget."

"No; he has a weak head that can only comprehend one thing at a time, but once he does comprehend it he clings to it steadily. He never forgets."

Katherine shook her head.

"I am not satisfied. Cochrane looked strangely at you as he quitted us. It was rash of you to venture upon speech with him at all. I trembled at every word you uttered more than when my brother seemed about to tear the disguise from me."

"I have had practise in the masques of the Louvre. I would what remains were as easily performed. I knew the hazard, and if it succeeded I counted that we were so much the safer."

"Whisht ye, whisht!" muttered the hostess, who was standing by the door listening; "there's some ane coming."

Katherine instantly resumed the pretence of baking, and Gordon again placed himself under the lantern.

The door was pushed open and Hislop appeared.

"The toon lads are making sport," he said. "They raised a cry enoo that ye were found, and hae drawn maist o' the folk tae the cross. But it's o' nae use to ye unless ye could rin out; and guid kens how that's to be managed, for there are twenty men guarding the house. I'm clean at my wits' ends how to serve you."

Gordon's brows contracted as he bent his head in meditation.

Katherine watched him eagerly, and with pulse quickened to pain.

Every outlet was guarded, and every hope of escape seemed to be extinguished. The only gleam of light which he could

perceive in the darkness that had fallen
upon them was the presence of his follower,
Muckle Will. But even his presence
inspired little confidence in the result
which was to follow their efforts! It was
impossible for two men to stand against
the band of Borderers who supported
Cochrane; and unless they could pass
them, there was no chance of escape.

They might have cut a way through the
midst of their foes had they been alone:
Gordon had made as bold a hazard before
now. But with a woman to conduct in
safety such a venture would have been
utter madness, even supposing Will had
the horses close at hand, which was exceedingly doubtful, seeing that he had neither
made himself known to the landlord, as he
had been directed, nor had explained why
he was there without the equipage.

A few seconds sufficed for him to make

this disagreeable review of their position. Then raising his head abruptly :

" Have you seen the fellow who was sleeping here a little while ago ? "

" Ay, he gaed out to the stable alang wi' the chiel ye had the tulzie wi' up the stair," said the host.

" He will betray you," said Katherine in agitation.

Lamington took her hands, gazing tenderly in her face.

" You will understand the lad some day, Kate ; meanwhile, be assured of this, I can trust him with my life, even as I could trust you."

" The Holy Mother grant that your trust be well placed," she said, still doubting.

" You will find it so," was his confident reply ; and turning to Hislop he continued, " When did the knave arrive ? "

" About twa hours syne."

" Had he no horses with him ?"

" He had nothing; he just came in, took a waught o' yull, and laid himself down there like a muckle sumph, and wadna say a word about where he cam' frae, or where he was going to, or anything ava."

Gordon's countenance lightened as if with some inspiration, and he hastily counted out ten gold pieces on the table.

" Thanks, host, for what you have done," he said, hurriedly; " and here is the reward I promised you doubled. You and your good dame shall hear from me again to your profit for this night's service, if I live."

Hislop iterated his readiness to serve so worthy a gentleman and so fair a lady, and wished that he saw them well through their trouble.

Katherine grasped her lover's arm, looking anxiously in his eyes as she observed him feel under his plaid for his sword, to make sure that it was ready to his hand.

"What are you about to do?" she queried.

"To make another venture; we must risk everything to win safe passage to our destination."

"But the risk need not be rashly made."

"Nothing but rashness can save us now. Have you courage, Katherine?"

"For your sake I think I have courage to dare anything."

"Then for my sake you must bide here for a little while. Should any one attempt to force you hence, blow upon this whistle; that will let me know your danger, and bring Will to your side."

"And you——?"

"I must go forth; and if I can but raise a riot among the burgesses we may escape unnoticed in the confusion. That is our only chance; and, by the saints, I think Cochrane himself supplies the means to help us to it. Stay you here, and do not stir till I return."

CHAPTER V.

THE COCHRANE PLACKS.

"Then whingers flew frae gentles' sides,
    And swords flew frae the shea's,
And red and rosy was the blood
    Ran doon the lily braes."

Katherine Janfarie.

E rushed out, making for the door which opened upon the High Street.

The sturdy Borderer, Fenwick, who was on guard, arrested him.

"You cannot pass, master, whatever your haste may be."

"I seek Sir Robert Cochrane," was the

5

response, in a hoarse, disguised voice, and with a manner of breathless haste; "and I must find him."

"If that be your errand, pass on. He was here a minute ago."

Lamington darted by the guard and speedily joined the crowd of burgesses who were flitting excitedly about the Town House, or standing together in groups, earnestly discussing the events of the night. Many of them carried links or lanterns, and the lights flashing through the darkness, and flickering under the strong wind which was sweeping up the street, imparted to their disturbed visages a gloomy aspect.

Gordon mingled amongst them, and much to his relief overheard dissatisfied murmurs at the untimely disturbance of the town's repose, for apparently so little purpose as the hunt after a brace of run-away lovers who could not be discovered.

" Know you who leads the Hot Trod ? " said Gordon to one stalwart fellow whom he heard swearing that he believed the whole affair was a trick of the Borderers to harry the town.

" I neither ken nor care," answered the man, surlily.

" It is Cochrane, the maker of the base placks—the fellow who has commanded us to accept pieces of lead and brass for good silver money, and who has ruined honest men by his knavery."

" I wish we could lay hands on the chiel; we'd let him ken what we think o' the Cochrane placks."

" After me, then, and you shall have your wish."

" Hey, lads, here's sport that's worth while turning out for," shouted the man to his comrades. " Wha'll take Cochrane placks in payment for his wark or guids ?"

"Nane of us," was the general yell of execration which rose at the mention of the debased coin.

"Let the maker of them ken that. Here's a chiel says that Cochrane himsel's among us the night. Come on, and gie him a taste of our mettle."

The proposition was greeted with a vehement shout that echoed from one end of the town to the other, and indicated the hearty detestation which was entertained for the king's favourite, in consequence of his ill-advised attempt to impose upon the people, in the matter of the new coin.

The crowd instantly followed Lamington towards the Royal Hunt; and as it passed onward the meaning of the new movement was hurriedly explained to neighbours and friends with all the exaggerations and transformations which a word passing rapidly from lip to lip in an excited mob assumes.

The crowd swelled as it progressed, and the original cause of the rising was entirely forgotten in the present and much more personal source of action.

The people had doggedly refused to accept the coin issued by Cochrane, trade had been interrupted in consequence, and much misery had been felt on that account in every town in Scotland. Merchants would not accept payment in the new coin for their goods, farmers would not take it for their grain, and labourers would not have it for their hire. The result was ruin to many men, starvation to many more, and discomfort to every one.

For these reasons the people entertained an intense hatred towards the man who had endeavoured to force the false coin upon them. And this sentiment was at any moment ready to assume a perilous expression wherever the king's favourite appeared, and any man bold enough to act as leader stood forward.

The happy remembrance of these circumstances promised now to afford Gordon and Katherine all the assistance of which they stood so much in need, and for which they could not have hoped from any other source.

His heart swelling with the consciousness of triumph, Gordon rushed onward raising the shout—

" Justice for the people—no more base placks ! "

The crowd pressed round the doors of the hostelry in spite of all the efforts to keep them back, made by the Borderers who had been left on guard.

The Borderers, unable to discover the meaning of the riot, formed inside the doorways with spears fixed in close phalanx, thereby checking the foremost of the crowd.

The people surged excitedly to and fro, and, still obeying the guidance of Lamington, called loudly for Sir Robert Cochrane, although they did not make any immediate attempt to break down the spears of the guard and force an entrance.

Suddenly there was a movement amongst the Borderers; they divided, leaving a passage for one man, and Sir Robert Cochrane, bearing a torch in his left hand, presented himself to the people.

The light shone full upon his stern visage, and the air of proud authority which he assumed, combined with the undaunted coolness with which he appeared unarmed before the men who summoned him so furiously, awed them for the moment, and made them silent.

"I am he you call Robert Cochrane," he said in a sharp, clear tone; "what is it you seek with me?"

A murmur like the distant roll of thunder passed along the crowd; but at first no one seemed to have courage enough to stand forward as spokesman, and singly to brave his contemptuous regard.

Lamington whispered in the ear of the man whom he had first addressed, and he immediately made a step in advance of his companions.

"Will ye tak' back the placks ye hae sent out to us made wi' brass and lead, and gie us guid silver to trade wi'?"

"The day I'm hanged they may be called in—not sooner," was the contemptuous retort.

"There's mony a true word spoke in jest, my lord," said the man threateningly.

"Stand aside, varlet; and all you who

hear me, take heed of what you do, for any violence offered to me in this matter is offered to the king himself, whose laws you break, and whose commands you disobey."

A crowd is as lightly moved as a feather, which goes any way the strongest current of wind blows it. Cochrane's calmness and audacity, and the authority with which he spoke, checked the impulse of the mob, which having no plan of action, was brought to a stand-still by his decisive answer.

There was another murmur and another pause; and during that pause Gordon heard the shrill note of the whistle which he had given to Katherine to sound in warning, if any danger assailed her during his absence. Before the note of alarm had done echoing through the house, his sword was in his hand.

" We shall have your promise, master,

to undo the cheat you have put upon us, nevertheless," he shouted, hoarsely.

The crowd caught up the shout with an eagerness that showed their sympathy in it, and their readiness to follow any leader in such a cause.

The whistle was still ringing in his ears, and he gave instant action to his words— an example which he knew the men behind him would follow if he led the way before their re-awakened sense of injury received any new check.

With a swift stroke of his sword he swept the torch out of Cochrane's hand. The suddenness of the movement had the advantage of preventing any of the Borderers observing who had struck the blow.

The crowd, now heaving and shouting with the fury of demons, pressed close behind him, and in its irresistible tide carried Cochrane away from the door. He struggled with might and main, but without effect. His loud cries for assistance were heard by Richard Janfarie, and he, raising the slogan of his father's house, pushed forward to the rescue, whilst his followers made a stout fight to support him.

As the men pushed their way out at the door, Lamington forced his way in. The excitement and confusion was too great for his movement to be observed.

Above all the tumult, his quick ear distinguished the voice of Katherine, and as he burst into the kitchen, he saw her struggling in the midst of half a dozen of her father's men.

Hislop was lying on the floor stunned; the hostess was using her nails furiously in trying to make one grim-visaged fellow relinquish his grasp of the lady whom the men were dragging towards the door.

When Lamington had quitted the kitchen, Katherine had waited in trembling impatience for the result of his adventure. For some minutes she had been undisturbed ; but at length she was startled by the sudden reappearance of Cochrane with six men. He had only had time to ask where the drover had gone when the tumultuous summons of the people had called him away.

He bade the men remain, however, and they asked for some ale, being fatigued with their long ride, and ready to make themselves comfortable at the first opportunity that offered.

The host produced a large can of ale, and Katherine, the better to sustain her character as an attendant, handed the mugs round to the men. One of them, being of a jovial mood, caught her hand.

" Come, sweeten the mug wi' your lips,

my lass," he said. "I'll barter my jack
and spear for a cradle, if yours be not a
fine face if that rag were off and both een
whole."

"If it was aff ye'd see a face that wad
scare ye, maister," she answered, forcing a
laugh, and trying to sustain her part,
although her limbs trembled under her;
for she knew that the man had seen her
frequently at Johnstone.

She trembled almost as much at the
thought of being detected in such a trivial
vulgar way by one of the common retainers,
after she had safely passed before the eyes
of her father and brother, as at the knowledge of her helpless position.

"A face to scare me!" he cried, with a
loud guffaw. "There's no a face o' man,
woman, or imp could do that; and I'll
prove it, whether ye are blind or no. I
ken a fresh lip when I see it."

He suddenly threw his arm round her neck. She started from him, and in doing so the bandage which had concealed one of her eyes and part of her face was lifted off by his bent arm.

The loud laugh with which the men had greeted their comrade's exploit became abruptly hushed when they heard him exclaim—

"Mistress Katherine herself, or I'm bewitched."

She attempted to re-cover her face, and to laugh the man out of his conviction. But he promptly bade one of his comrades summon the master of Johnstone and Sir Robert Cochrane, whilst he seized her by the arm. She instantly gave the signal with all her might, and Hislop sprang to the door to prevent any one passing. He had a sharp tussle with three of the men until a heavy blow on the head with a spear-staff laid him insensible on the floor.

Meanwhile Katherine, assisted by the dame, had been struggling to release herself, and to repeat the signal. Thus she was when Gordon came to the rescue.

A glance showed him the position of affairs.

Her cry of joy at his appearance turned the attention of her captors to him, and four spears were instantly levelled at his breast.

Parrying the thrust of the foremost, he cut the man down, and springing to one side, gripped a second by the throat, and hurled him over his fallen comrade with such force that his head striking on the floor, he was stunned. The other two made furious lounges, which were dexterously warded, and by another sudden spring he closed with the third man. The fourth, however, as if prepared for this movement, suddenly dropped his spear and drew his whinger, with which he would be able to assist his comrade better at close quarters.

At the same time the man who had recognized Katherine relinquished his hold of her, and sprang forward with his short sword upraised to strike Gordon on the back.

Katherine screamed as she saw the weapon uplifted, whilst Gordon, engaged with the two men before him, was unaware of his peril.

A huge shadow darkened the doorway, and the uplifted arm fell broken and power-less to the man's side, under the blow of a heavy staff wielded by the muscular hand of Will Craig. Another blow laid the man prone on the floor.

"I heard the whistle, and I thought

there was something wrang," muttered Will, without pausing in his onslaught.

Gordon had disengaged himself from his two assailants, and both fell under the sledge-hammer blows of Will's staff. The last man—the one who had retained hold of Katherine—seeing how matters stood, made a bold rush for the door, and just as he was crossing the threshold received such a blow from Will's cudgel on the buttocks as lifted him a step forward on his way, and sent him out of the house howling.

" Where are the horses ? " cried Gordon.

" On the ither side o' the water. The brig's guarded, but I hae a boat. Come on, They're fechting like deils outside, and winna see us."

Lamington took Katherine by the hand ; her strength had been severely tried, but she was able to hasten with him out of the

6

house and run to the river side, as the
Borderers under Sir Hugh Janfarie galloped down from the Grey Friar to the
rescue of Sir Robert Cochrane.

CHAPTER VI.

THE RIOT.

"My blessing on your heart, sweet thing,
    Wae to your wilful will;
There's many a gallant gentleman
    Whae's blood you have garr'd to spill."
                            Katherine Janfurie.

THE clamour of the riot rose upon the night like the roar of an angry sea. The clang of arms, the tramp of horses' hoofs, the wild shriek of the death-smitten, the infuriated yell of the avenger, the loud shouts of the Borderers, and all the confusion of noises which a tempest of the fiercest of human

passions produces, merged into one long
thunderous roar.

The tide surged wildly, as now the
Borderers were beaten back and again
made good their ground with the dogged
valour of men whose trade is strife.

The sound of the tumult echoed along
the valley of the Nith and startled the
monks of Lin-Cluden in their midnight
vigils, and possibly alarmed a few of the
good men who were softening the austerities of their order with some stolen
indulgence.

In the town, lights flashed everywhere.
Presently the beacon fire on the tower of
the castle was kindled, and was soon
answered by signals from the surrounding heights and peels. The petty riot,
which had been so lightly raised, had
now swelled into the proportions of a
battle.

Sir Hugh Janfarie, with the main detachment of his followers, rode down upon the combatants. He encountered Musgrave, who explained as clearly as he could the source of the quarrel; and Sir Hugh, sensible of the danger of the Hot Trod being arrested in consequence of the brawl, and of the probable reprisals the townsfolk would make for what harm befel them, rode into the hottest of the fight, endeavouring to allay its fury.

But his words were unheard in the prevailing turmoil, and his purpose was misunderstood. The result of his attempted peace-making was to increase the blind rage of the burgesses.

Nicol, with the emblem of the Hot Trod, rode close by his father. But the spear was wrenched from his grasp, and the burning sod was trampled underfoot; at that the townsfolk raised a deafening cheer, renewing the assault more vigorously than before.

They had many old scores to settle with the Borderers, and they were not sorry to find so favourable an opportunity to settle some of them. Besides, blood had been already spilled on both sides, and Janfarie's mediation, which might have been of service a little while ago, came too late when the men were heated with action and thirsting to avenge fallen comrades.

There was nothing for the Borderers to do but keep close together and beat as dignified a retreat as the circumstances permitted.

Sir Hugh and Nicol cut their way through the crowd to the side of Cochrane and Richard, who were receiving rough usage from a band of stout fellows, and were being dragged towards the Town House.

The rescue was effected by a bold dash and a fierce hacking down of every man who attempted to bar the way of the old knight to his son and friend. One fellow, who wielded a Jeddart axe with strength and address, made a sturdy stand, and several times planted his blows with such force, that, but for the careering of the horse, he would have stricken the knight to the ground. As if determined not to be foiled, he sprang at the horse's head, gripped the bridle, and swinging the axe, brought it down with violence. But Sir Hugh, bending forward, avoided the blade of the axe by receiving the blow of the shaft on his shoulder. The blow had been given with so much force that the shaft snapped in twain, the blade falling harmlessly to the ground.

Before the man could regain his balance, or do more than utter a howl of chagrin at the adroitness which had foiled his effort, Sir Hugh pierced him through the neck, and he fell with a groan beneath the horse's feet.

"My father!" shrieked a voice as the man fell. The next instant a youth of about eighteen years sprang with the agility and fury of a wild cat upon Sir Hugh, and with a sharp souter's knife, stabbed him under the sword arm, which was at the moment upraised.

The youth was beaten down by the prickers' spears, and trampled upon by their horses.

At the spectacle of this swift retaliation on both sides, there arose a yell from the townsfolk, wilder and more terrible than any that had yet added its discord to the raging elements of the night. There was a pause, too, like the momentary stillness which precedes the crash of a thunderbolt.

Then it came; a body of men drew close together, and at a swinging trot, with arms in rest, advanced upon the Borderers. Steadily they moved with teeth set, and in silence that seemed more terrible than the wildest outcries.

Sir Hugh, on receiving the wound, had fallen forward on the neck of his horse, and would have fallen had not Richard struggled to his side in time to steady him in the saddle.

" You are hurt, sir," he said agitatedly.

" Avenge me," was the grim answer of the knight.

Richard sprang upon the horse behind him, and taking a firm hold of his sword belt, contrived to hold him on the seat whilst he snatched the sword from his father's now powerless hand, and with it met the determined onslaught of the towns-men.

" Steady, lads," shouted Cochrane, "and withdraw to the bridge. There you will be able to hold your ground against the whole town of rebellious loons."

The Borderers formed in double line and began to move slowly backward, contesting every inch of ground.

"It is my father's sword," muttered Richard Janfarie between his clenched teeth; "and this night I will prove myself worthy to bear it."

Instead of retreating with his company, he touched the horse with his heels, and burst into the midst of the advancing foe, hewing them down right and left with such fury that he cleared a space and threw them into some confusion.

But the crowd formed a circle round him, cutting him off from his friends, who were unaware of his danger.

Observing this, he made the horse wheel

round, and again fought his way through the mass, wielding the long sword of his father with all the pith his thirst for vengeance inspired.

The people fell back more astounded by the strange sight of the double burden of the horse—one man apparently dead, and the other animated as if with the rage of a demon—more awed by this even than his prowess.

They fell before him, they shrank from him, and the confusion caused by his single assault materially aided the Borderers in reaching the bridge with unbroken line.

There the conflict was brought to a sudden cessation by the appearance of a band of the Grey Friars, who, headed by their Superior, and each carrying a flaming torch which revealed his holy order, marched boldly between the opposing lines of Borderers and townsmen, at the moment when, exhausted and wounded, Richard Janfarie rejoined his comrades.

Mad as the people were with the events which had transpired, they came to a halt before the stern glances of the Friars.

The Superior commanded silence, and the uproar gradually subsided like the diminishing sound of an ebbing tide.

When silence had been obtained the monk demanded an explanation of the outrage upon the town's repose.

Twenty voices attempted to answer him at once, but the Superior motioned them to silence as Sir Robert Cochrane advanced and made himself known.

He briefly explained the purpose of the Borderers' entrance into the town, and the manner in which the riot had been raised by some foolish demands of the people, made to him as a servant of the king at that inopportune time, and with unmannerly threats.

"How his Majesty may think of this matter when it is explained to him," he added in conclusion, "I cannot say. But this much I may tell you, that I believe that the disturbance was raised in the first place by the rascal we are pursuing, in order to cover his own escape."

"Who is the man?" queried the monk.

"Bertrand Gordon, called Laird of Lamington."

"Have you arrested him?"

"No; but he cannot be far hence, and we must crave your protection whilst we continue our search, and leave our wounded to your care."

The Superior bowed in acquiescence, saying:

"As you know the man, you will be able to make him answer for his share in this disturbance."

"By the Sacred Mother of Heaven,"

cried Janfarie in a hollow voice, " he shall answer that to me. My father is dead, and to Lamington I look for an account of his fate."

The young man had lifted the body from the horse, purposing to staunch his wound, when he had discovered that no aid of his could serve him, and he was now kneeling over his dead father as he made his vow of retaliation.

Nicol was by his brother's side. Grief choked him, and he could not speak ; but he pressed Richard's hand, in token that he shared in his resolve.

The torches flickering and wavering in the wind shed a red glare over the crowd, and gleamed upon the breast of the rapid flowing Nith as it sped onward to the Solway, the stream beating against the arches of the bridge as they impeded its course, and murmuring a melancholy song, that at the moment seemed like a dirge for the dead knight.

The light shone upon the grey-hooded monks; upon the gloomy visages of the defeated Borderers as they stood wounded, holding by the croups of their saddles, or sat motionless in their seats with thoughts of dire vengeance in their hearts. The lights flashed on the now anxious faces of the townsfolk as they stood in breathless awe at the weird sound the man's voice had made, and already abashed by the memory of what had occurred.

The sudden pause in the uproar which had been rampant only a moment before, the unsteady light cast over all by the flaming links, and the stillness of the night—for the very wind seemed to have become hushed—imparted a solemnity to the wild scene, and to the vow which had just been spoken that subdued the passions of the men, and held them as if spell-bound.

The eerie pause was broken by Richard Janfarie starting to his feet, and directing his followers to carry their chief to the monastery.

In grim silence a litter of spears was formed, and the body of the dead knight placed upon it. In grim silence the men with their sad burthen, headed by four monks as torch-bearers, passed through the crowd which made way for them, and marched up the street to the monastery.

Then the people slowly turned to the mournful task of seeking their wounded and dead friends. Low moans and bitter shrieks of anguish disturbed the night, as wives, mothers, and sweethearts, now rushing forth from their homes, encountered friends bearing the lifeless remains of those who were dearest to them, or recognized the mainstay of their households lying disabled on the street. It was a sad night's work for the bonnie town of Dumfries; and many hearts ached with the memory of it long afterward. One of its saddest incidents was connected with the man who had so desperately assaulted Sir Hugh, and whose fall had been the main instrument of the knight's death. His wife found her husband and son both slain, and hideously disfigured by horses' hoofs. With shrieks of despair she threw herself upon the mangled bodies, kissing their clotted lips, and calling to them by name to rise.

She had to be forced away by some kindly neighbours, who said that her reason was affected. The man had been a good husband, and the son who had wrought such swift retribution for his father's fall had been her only bairn.

As soon as the body of Sir Hugh had been lifted up, Cochrane grasped Richard's arm.

"We cannot halt in the pursuit," he said; "we must leave till we return what marks of respect we owe your father."

"I am ready," answered Janfarie, dourly.

"Pick a dozen of your best men, then, to accompany us. The fewer we are the more lightly we will follow the track. I will not pause in the chase till he is captured."

"I shall not pause in the chase till he is dead," was Janfarie's hollow response.

"Let it be such a death as he merits— not that of honourable folk, but the gibbet of a felon."

"It shall be the worst that I can find for him when the hour comes."

Cochrane clasped his hand, peering in

his face with a strange vicious glitter in his eyes.

"Let me guide your choice," he said, greedily. "I know his spirit, and I know where to strike him deepest. Let me guide your choice in the atonement you would wreak upon him, and I promise you that you shall see him degraded, spurned, and mocked at by those whose esteem he values most — ay, by Saint Andrew, even by Mistress Katherine herself. Then let him swing on the highest tree at hand."

Janfarie caught the venomous glitter of the man's eyes, and he did not altogether relish it, embittered though he was to the last degree against the subject of their conversation.

"Such retribution as you purpose would be worth tarrying for; but I can promise nought save this, that there is no torture I would not put him to."

" Enough. The memory of your father will keep your purpose steady."

" That memory will feed my hate while I have power to lift a hand."

Here Nicol, who had been scouring the streets for stray or wounded followers, rushed up to his brother.

" We have missed them again," he shouted. " They have crossed the river in a boat."

" Who gave you these tidings ? "

" This fellow who has had a tussle with Lamington, and who followed them to the river bank."

" Get your men together," said Cochrane hastily to Janfarie; " we may have them before the night is out yet. You, Nicol, must hie to Linlithgow with tidings of this treachery to his Majesty. We shall have the highest authority of the land for what we do."

" By your leave, I would rather continue in the chase," rejoined Nicol, disappointed by the prospect of being removed from his share in the pursuit.

Cochrane answered him with an air of persuasive confidence, which flattered the youth and modified his disappointment.

" Nay, but you must submit to this for all our sakes. There is no other I can trust to bear my message to the king, and it is from him only that I care to seek assistance in this matter. There are other reasons besides that his Majesty should have early knowledge of this outrage."

" Musgrave or Fenwick might go," said Nicol, still hesitating ; they are my seniors, and therefore better qualified to report the affair to his Majesty."

Cochrane placed his hand on Nicol's shoulder and whispered :

" Ay, but there is a missive that must be placed in the king's own hand, and I would trust it to none other save you. Will you serve me ? "

" Since there is no help for it, I will."

" I shall owe you much for this service, and I may have the power to pay it sooner than you hope—trust me."

A few minutes sufficed for Cochrane to give his now willing carrier the needful instructions and the packet of which he had spoken. By that time Janfarie had selected his men, had got the leash of hounds together, and arms had been examined.

When Cochrane joined the party the gates of the bridge were opened, and they rode across in double file at a smart canter. The pale starlight gleamed upon their steel caps, and the bridge gave out a hollow sound under the horses' hoofs. They rode steadily, and without a word passing amongst them.

Every man was conscious that he was engaged in a hunt which was to end only at the death at the quarry.

CHAPTER VII.

THE PRIORY OF KELLS.

"Sublime is the faith of a lonely soul,
In pain and trouble cherished;
Sublime the spirit of hope that lives,
When earthly hope has perished."
PROF. WILSON, *Isle of Palms.*

THE riot had been at its height when Lamington, with Katherine, had followed Will Craig to the bank of the river where he had the boat moored at a point nearly opposite the water-gate of the monastery. They were unaware that any had observed their flight. But the man who had received

Will's last blow had seen them, had followed them at a safe distance, and so
had been able to give intelligence of their
route.

They embarked; Will pulled across the
stream, his giant arms making the oars fly
through the water, and carrying the boat a
little way up the stream in spite of the
strong current.

He pulled to the shore through a thick
bed of rushes at the western end of a short
row of houses which formed the nucleus of
Maxweltown.

The motion of the boat and the keen
breeze blowing upon her cheeks had re-
vived the lady, and she was able to spring
lightly to the land. Lamington led her
up the bank and then waited for Will, who
had stayed to make fast the boat to a huge
stone, having explained that he had found
it there, and " didna want the owner to be

ony the waur for the liberty he had taen wi' his cockleshell."

The tumult on the other side was ringing in their ears, and Katherine clung closely to her lover, disturbed by the wild sounds she heard, although she knew that they insured their present safety.

" Come on this gate now, maister," cried Will, taking the direction of Lincluden.

" Where are the horses?" queried the master.

" Stark's got them safe eneuch."

Almost as he spoke, he darted into a thicket of trees; and in a small open space the fugitives saw two powerful horses tied to the branch of a tree, whilst a huge black hound sat on his haunches gravely watching them.

That was Stark. The hound sprang up joyfully at the sight of Will, and encountered him with wagging tail.

"It's a' richt," muttered Will. "Stark never wags his tail when onybody has been interferin' wi' him."

As Gordon looked to the girths of the saddles he angrily inquired why the man had left the horses there instead of bringing them to the hostelry.

The big, simple-looking fellow, who had the heart of a brave gentleman and the mind of a child, scratched his head, looked puzzledly at his master, then looked imploringly at Katherine, and, last of all, gazed down inquiringly at the upturned face of his dog.

"Now, what would ye say to that, Stark?" he said, scratching away at his head. The hound cocked his ears and bent his head a little to one side, as if, with a species of human intelligence, he were considering the problem set before him.

At any other moment Katherine would

have been amused by the equal degree of gravity on the faces of man and dog.

"Now, I just speir at you, Stark," Will continued, " what would ye say ?   He tells me to be siccar and secret, and I thought that I couldna be half sae secret wi' twa horses at my heels as I could be my lane. Sae I leave ye here to tak' care o' the brutes, and that's siccar ; and syne I gang mysel' ower the watter, stealing a boat to do that, sae that nae questions should be speired at the brig, and I wait at the hostel without saying a word to mortal body, and I count a' that secret.   But what do you think, Stark, for a' that he is angry wi' me, and says I am a gouk ? "

"Tut, man," said Lamington, who, know-his servitor's ways, could barely restrain a smile even at that moment of peril, " the horses would not have told any one your business."

"Na ; but folk would hae seen them and speired about them, and would maybe hae kenned what airt they cam' frae. Eh, Stark ?"

The hound wagged his tail as if in assent, and Muckle Will—as he was called on account of his huge frame—closed one of his eyes with an expression of great cunning, but it was a very simple sort of look for all that.

"Do not blame him," said Katherine ; "he has served us well despite his mistake. We owe our present safety greatly to him."

"Will is not afraid of my anger, and in truth there is more reason in his explanation than I expected. I am glad you have so soon come to know his worth ; for, after you, Katherine, there is no one I would not rather lose than this simple fellow. Come hither, Will."

The tall, broad-shouldered simpleton advanced at the bidding, the hound marching beside him.

Katherine laid her hand on his arm.

" If your master is not in the humour to do it, Will, I thank you for the good service you have done us."

The giant hung his head, abashed by her earnestness, and removing his bonnet, began to swing it awkwardly in his hands.

" Look up, Will," said his master ; " look well at this lady that you may know her, for you must serve her as truly in all things as you would serve me."

As every sentiment, as well as his service, was at the command of his master, Will's bashfulness disappeared. He looked steadily at the lady's face, which the starlight revealed to him. Then he said shyly—

" Ye are a bonnie lady, and Stark and

me will serve you truly. See what he says ; speak for yoursel', Stark. Speak to the lady, and tell her ye'll do her bidding."

The hound walked round Katherine twice, and then, stopping beside her, laid his head on her hand. She patted him, and the dog wagged his tail in joyful acknowledgment.

" That's a' richt," said Will, " Stark and you will be great friends, and by the same rule you and me will be great friends."

Apparently satisfied with that compact, the giant led the horses out of the thicket.

Lamington wrapped the drover's plaid round Katherine, assisted her to mount one of the horses, and sprang on to the other himself.

" Follow, Will, with what speed you may, to the Priory of Kells. You know our pursuers ; take heed that none of them lay hold of you."

" Aye, weel, they wad just hae to let go again," was Will's resigned response.

The horses started, and Will with his hound watched them until they had disappeared amongst the black shadows of the wood which belted the road for several miles.

Then he gripped his heavy cudgel tightly, and followed at a swinging pace, sustaining a lively conversation with Stark all the time. It was like the prattle with which a child is accustomed to commune with its pets ; but through it all there were flashes of shrewdness which would have suggested that the man was amusing himself, rather than giving vent to his natural character.

The horses upon which the fugitives were now mounted were fresh, and stretched to their work with spirit. They swept by the Abbey of Lincluden in which the vestal light was burning and shedding a spectral gleam through the trees. They sped down the valley, and through the glens by Lochinkit. Then skirting Upper Bar and Crogo, they rose upon the high land; and the white crested heads of the Galloway hills became visible against the horizon.

The country stretched like a rolling sea before them. Now they rose upon the brow of some bare height, with the dark highlands looming up before them; again they were closed in the hollow of some bossy glen, the darkness lending fantastic shapes to jutting boulders of rock, or waving ash, or stunted thorn, with the sound of gurgling water making a weird melody in the night.

But over all there was an eerie sense of silence caught from the grand solitude of the hills.

There were streams and rivers to cross, morasses to avoid, and treacherous precipices, whose lips were concealed by furze and heather, to evade. But a keen eye, a steady hand, and sure-footed horses, carried the fugitives safely through all the journey.

At length the dim outline of the Forest of Kells became perceptible. The forest had been erected into a royal hunting-ground by the Bruce, and was a favourite resort of the Scottish monarchs for the pleasures of the chase. The memory of its ancient glory is still preserved in several of its local names. Tradition, too, has much of interest to tell of the Druid stones which lie upon the surrounding heights; the murder holes which are found in the table lands, and which were anciently used by the barons who had the right of putting offenders to death by pit and gibbet—that is, by drowning and smothering them in the pits, or hanging them on the nearest tree— and of the old wall called the Deil's Dyke.

The Priory of Kells was a small establishment, which had been given in free alms to the Archdeacon of Galloway by Robert Bruce, and which obtained some importance as an occasional resting-place of the royal party when engaged in the chase. The building stood at one of the mouths of the forest; it was square and bare, but it had the strength of a feudal tower.

When the fugitives drew rein at the gate, the bell was sounding for early matins; but it was some time before Lamington's summons was answered.

The gatekeeper at length showed himself, and Lamington announced that he was there by tryst with the Abbot Panther. That name having been repeated, the man opened the gate. The visitors were conducted across a grass court to the entrance to the Prior's house.

There the mention of the Abbot's name
had the effect of procuring them immediate
admission.   They were conducted to a
small waiting-room with bare walls and a
small grated window.   It was lit by a
small cruzie, standing in a niche in the
wall, and furnished with a couple of chairs
and a reading-desk.   They had not to wait
long.   A hooded monk appeared, and led
Gordon to the presence of the Abbot, whilst
Katherine was left alone.

The same monk again entered the waiting-room after the lapse of a little time,
bearing a lighted cruzie in his hand.   He
beckoned the lady to follow him, and she
obeyed.

They passed along a narrow corridor, the
bare grey walls of which, feebly illumed by
the lamp in the monk's hand, looked so
cold and dismal that it was more like the
hall of a prison than that of the residence
of a church dignitary.

They ascended a narrow staircase and entered another passage similar to the first. At the farther end of this passage the monk threw open a door.

"This is your chamber, sister; here you may rest for the present," said the monk.

He handed the light to her, and without waiting for any thanks or question, departed with noiseless steps.

Although Katherine was sorely bewildered by the manner of her monkly chamberlain, and by the continued absence of her lover, she made no effort to satisfy her curiosity; for she was too much fatigued by her journey and too much awed by the grimness of the place and the solemn stillness pervading it—a stillness broken only by the subdued chant of the monks at their morning exercise in the Priory Chapel. She entered the chamber

and closed the door.   Like the other apartments she had seen, the walls were bare ;
the furniture consisted of a table with a
missal, a priedieu and a crucifix, and a low
narrow couch.   After an earnest supplication for pardon for whatever error she had
committed, and for the happiness of those
from whom she had fled, she laid herself,
dressed as she was, on the couch.   Sleep
soon brought a blissful oblivion to all the
anxieties and fatigues of the night.

* * * * *

The sun gleamed in through the narrow
window of Katherine's chamber and she
wakened wearily from her sleep.   She had
been dreaming of her brother Richard—
dreaming that he had come to her dressed
in a shroud, and had stretched forth skeleton
hands towards her warningly.

She lay half awake now, her eyes twink-
ling under the ray of sunlight that was

crossing them, and fancying that she heard her brother's voice pronouncing her name. The sound echoed strangely in her ears, and in a half conscious way she tried to argue with herself that the sound existed only in her dream. But it was suddenly repeated with such sharp emphasis that with a smothered cry she sprang from the couch.

Her startled eyes became fixed upon Richard Janfarie who stood by the door, pale and worn by exertion, but with a stern, relentless expression that chilled her blood. More, however, than his stern visage, more than the surprise of discovering him there, her eyes were attracted and her mind appalled by the black badge which he wore on his right arm. A thousand wild fancies flashed upon her mind at once, but none explained the meaning of that grim badge; her heart beat quick and her limbs trembled as she gazed alternately upon it and the man's face.

He remained silent, as if conscious of her torturing doubts, and willing to leave her to them for a space.

She roused herself with a violent effort, and pointing with trembling finger to his badge, she spoke in a terrified whisper:

"Why do you wear that?"

He advanced a step into the apartment, and halted in a position which permitted the rays of the sun to fall directly on his arm.

"I wear this for our father," he said, slowly.

"My father!" she cried, while she sprang towards him and grasped his arm; "is he dead?"

Richard shook her hand from him with the scorn of one who feels that he is polluted by a touch.

" Ay, he is dead—he has been murdered ;
and you, mistress, and Lamington are his
assassins."

The scorn with which he had flung her
from him made her shrink back a pace with
tingling cheeks. His scorn she would
have resented, but the accusation he had
made struck her speechless. She stood
mutely gazing at him, unable to realize the
full import of his words.

Her silence enraged him.

" Are you so callous that you are not
moved even by the tidings of the foul work
which has been done ? Are you so heartless
that even your father's murder cannot make
you sensible of your shame ? "

" My father dead—and by foul work !"
she muttered, absently, and in a low tone
of anguish ; " and you charge Lamington
with the crime—oh, you are mad, Richard !
or you are trying to frighten me that you

may force me to yield myself to Robert Cochrane."

And she sank upon the couch, covering her face with her hands and sobbing bitterly.

"I have no need to frighten you to yield to your husband. He is here with power to enforce his right to control you; and I am here to conduct you to the Abbot's Court, where you will learn your duty from fitter lips than mine, and where you shall have proofs of Lamington's guilt."

CHAPTER VIII.

THE SUMMONS.

"Upraise she trembling frae her seat,
    And tottered like to fa';
Her cheek grew like the rose, and then
    Turned whiter than the snaw."

Lady Jean.

DISTRAUGHT by the declaration of her brother, doubting its truth, and yet compelled to give it credence by the bitter earnestness of his manner, Katherine sat dumbly looking at him. Her sobs had ceased now; for, although the first sharp pangs the intelligence of her father's death caused her had wrung from her a woman's tears, the grave charge which accompanied the tidings, and the intimation of Cochrane's presence for the purpose of enforcing his hateful claims, stirred the spirit of resistance within her, and for the moment grief was overcome by indignation.

Still there was an undercurrent of contending emotions which she could not control. Her heart revolted from the bare thought of the guilt attributed to Lamington, whilst it was filled with anguish at the consciousness that by whatever hand her father had fallen, her flight had led him to his death. Besides, Gordon had been some time away from her while they had been at the hostelry in Dumfries, and sorely pressed by her father's followers, obliged to strike for his own life, it was possible that in the darkness or in the confusion of the struggle his hand might have stricken the fatal blow. That was the doubt which lingered in her mind and constrained her indignation. It weakened her, notwithstanding the strength she obtained from her conviction of Lamington's innocence in intention at least, and from the shuddering repugnance with which she had now come to regard the very name of Cochrane.

She rose slowly from the couch, her hands clasped, and her features fixed. But she made no movement to approach her brother. She spoke in a low soft tone, in which there was a piteous chord of pain.

"You give me sad news, brother—the sadder in that if it be true my father is dead, I am robbed of the hope I held that one day I would satisfy him and our dear mother—and all of you that in my disobedience I had spared you much misery."

Her evident distress was not without its

effect upon him, for Janfarie had a kindly
regard for his sister, although he could not
pardon the measure she had taken to
thwart the designs and aspirations of their
house.   He had all his mother's ambition,
and Cochrane had proffered him the opportunity to carry that ambition to its
highest bent.   His mind had been dazzled
by the prospect thus presented to him;
and in proportion to the brilliance of the
prospect he was blinded to the real nature
of the magician who presented it, whilst
he became insensible to the tenderer and
nobler feelings which had driven his sister
to rebellion.   He saw in her conduct only
the perversity of a silly woman, and so he
made answer harshly:

"Then you will satisfy us that we have
all been fools, and yours the only head
with a grain of wisdom amongst us.   Your
shame will serve us to good purpose if it
can do that."

She winced; her brow became flushed and her eyes kindled, but she spoke sadly:

"You have driven me to what error I may have done. You counted it no sacrifice to make me the price of a knave's favour. In spite of every prayer and appeal I made, you dragged me to the altar. You took no thought of the years of agony to which you were dooming me; you took no thought of the death to which you condemned me when you told me I was his wife; for if my loathing for the bonds you had thrust upon me—if Robert Cochrane's touch had not been enough to kill me, my own hand would have released me."

"I would have pitied you had you been released so; but now you have made yourself a thing of scorn."

"You will learn to think otherwise yet, Richard. At present you are smarting

under the memory of our father's death;
you do not see that Cochrane has cajoled
you—that he is fooling you."

"By the saints, if I thought that,"
muttered Janfarie, frowning darkly, and
then checking himself; "but shame upon
me to give ear to such words from a mad
wench who has disgraced her family for
the sake of a popinjay. Attend me, mistress, to the Abbot's court without more
delay."

"I will attend you presently," she
answered, quietly; "give me a moment to
prepare myself for this trial—for such I
count the interview to which you command
me is to be."

Janfarie turned on his heel and withdrew, taking his stand outside the door to
guard against any attempt of his sister to
elude him.

After a moment's pause, during which

she looked dazedly at the closed door, she threw herself upon her knees on the priedieu, and bowing her head low she raised her clasped hands in supplication.

She had maintained her composure during the presence of her brother; but now that she was alone all the contending emotions of her breast struggled for utterance, and overwhelmed her. The death of her father, the accusation of Lamington, and the consciousness of her own share in these miserable events, supplied her with bitter thoughts, for which there was no outlet save in prayer.

She seemed calmer when she regained her feet, and able to think of the more immediate necessities of the occasion. She hastily removed the garments which the friendly hostess of the Royal Hunt had supplied for her disguise; and as they had been only thrown over her own dress, she

9

had merely to cast them aside to appear in apparel more becoming her position, although its bravery was still in sad contrast to the circumstances surrounding her.

She adjusted her bodice, and the skirts which had been tucked up. Then with her hands she smoothed her hair as well as she could with such primitive toilet instruments, and without a mirror; for, woman-like, she wished to present herself in as becoming a guise as possible before the Abbot, upon whose word all her future happiness and the very life of her lover seemed at this moment to depend.

Slight as the change was, it was enough with her natural charms to transform a rustic lass into a dignified lady. She had need of all her courage to meet the emergency calmly. When she joined her brother, it was with a bearing of quiet dignity that was not without its effect even upon him.

He conducted her to the basement of the building, and as she passed along the hall, one of the windows permitted her a glimpse of the horses and the Borderers waiting in the square without.

She experienced a thrill of dismay, as this discovery reminded her of the power against which she had to do battle.

Her brother, however, was not permitted to observe anything of the alarm she felt. Her features remained pale and almost rigid.

The chamber in which the Abbot had appointed to hold his impromptu court was the principal one of the Priory; and as it belonged to the suite set apart for the king during his sojourn in the forest, it was furnished with some taste, and even with a degree of luxury. It had six windows of a larger size than any others in the building, and the recesses which they formed displayed the great thickness of the walls. In these recesses, and immediately beneath the casements, were stone seats long enough to accommodate three persons. The walls were hung with tapestry, and a number of couches and chairs covered with velvet gave the apartment a rich and comfortable appearance, which was almost enough to have caused one who had been tarrying in the other apartments of the Priory to think that he had suddenly stepped out of the cold regions of poverty into those of wealth.

Between the central windows was placed, on a slightly-raised platform, a huge oaken chair, curiously carved and surmounted by a mitre and a crown. The seat and back were covered with ruby silk. As if to subdue the light admitted by the first windows on the right and left of this chair, heavy curtains were drawn across them. By this means the face of the person who might occupy this seat of honour was almost entirely concealed from those who might stand before him, whilst every change in their countenances would be revealed by the light which fell full upon them.

Entering this apartment from the dim passages which she had traversed, Katherine's eyes were dazzled by the sun's rays, so that for an instant the place seemed to be unoccupied. But presently her eyes became accustomed to the light, and she observed a man advancing towards her from the shadow of one of the curtained windows.

She drew back as she recognized Cochrane.

Her movement was one of repugnance,

not of fear; and Sir Robert noting and
comprehending it, halted with brows knit,
and his cunning eyes fixed searchingly
upon her.

"You have given us a long ride,
madam," he said, politely, but with an
air of severity; "I trust that you may be
sufficiently fatigued by this time to be in a
humour to listen to the counsels of those
whose honour you are debasing, and to
whom you are bound by most solemn
bonds."

With a shudder of disgust she turned
sharply upon her brother.

"You summoned me hither to meet the
lord Abbot," she said, haughtily, "and
your trick has served you so far that it
has brought me unprotected into this man's
presence; but it can serve you no further.
Stand aside, Richard Janfarie, and let me
pass."

She spoke with so much dignity and authority that her brother appeared to hesitate.

" Stand aside," she repeated, " you are no friend of mine. I now understand the lies with which you have alarmed me ; and my word upon it, brother, I am as full of sorrow to know you the base instrument of this man as I am full of shame for the extremity to which you have forced me."

" I have spoken truth in all that I have said, as you will soon discover," he answered, gloomily.

Before she could make any comment a signal from Cochrane caused her brother to retire, closing the door behind him, and locking it as she knew by the click the bolt made in shooting into the lock.

" Richard—brother, do not leave me— for the Sacred Mother's sake do not leave me with him," she cried, running to the door and vainly attempting to force it open.

Her efforts to escape were futile, and her cries were unanswered.

Cochrane, as if perfectly secure in his position, waited patiently until she had exhausted her attempts to open the door. Then he advanced, and courteously, but with firm bearing, conducted her to a couch and bade her be seated.

She saw that opposition was useless, and she submitted, waiting with considerable trepidation the upshot of this interview into which she had been trepanned, but wearing upon her brow a flush of indignation which concealed her fears and rather added to the beauty of her countenance than otherwise.

CHAPTER IX.

AT BAY.

" And he has gained my mother's ear—
My father's stern command ;
Yet this fond heart can ne'er be his,
Although he claim my hand."

Lady Jean.

OCHRANE paused, as if to give her time to collect herself. His manner was that of extreme courtesy, and the sneering smile to which his lips were so well accustomed had entirely given place to an expression of grave concern. He remained standing before her, his hands lightly crossed behind him, whilst he scanned her features narrowly.

"Now, madam," he said at length, "now that our game at hide-and-seek is brought to a close, and that we are alone together, we have an opportunity of coming to an understanding."

He spoke in a very low tone, as if afraid of any one overhearing him; but indeed it was his custom at all times to speak in a very mellow, persuasive voice.

"That understanding is soon reached," she rejoined, firmly. "You have forced upon me an honour, Sir Robert Cochrane, which you were well aware was loathsome to me. I have surely proved my scorn for it; and now I seek only an audience of the Abbot to obtain release from whatever bonds my helplessness permitted you to fasten upon me."

She partly rose, but a movement of his hand warned her to remain seated.

"The bonds you speak of, mistress, are

not so lightly broken as you would seem
to think. That you will test for yourself.
His lordship will be here presently, and
you shall learn from his lips the truth of
what I say."

"Till then, sir, spare me your presence."

"I have no wish to intrude it upon you
further than the circumstances warrant.
But before his lordship comes—before you
compel me to use the last measures to
bring you to a sense of duty, I would fain
try gentler means to make you feel that
your own happiness, and that of those who
should be dear to you, is endangered by
your wilfulness."

"I have decided, sir, which way my
happiness lies, and no words of yours will
move me."

Her contempt, expressed in every tone
and look, did not disturb him; he remained
to the last degree resolutely polite, and he

even affected a tone of regret which made his conduct appear less cruel than it otherwise would have done.

"It is, madam, because I respect your judgment that I have insisted upon this interview. You must hear me."

"Since your courtesy leaves me no option, I listen," she said, sarcastically.

"That is well for all our sakes. You must first understand my real position in the events which have so stirred your ire against me. Since it is likely to displease you, I would say nothing of the regard for you with which your—will you permit me to say it?—beauty inspired me, and more even than that, the deep respect with which I was filled in discovering the high qualities of your mind. Of all this I would say nothing, so anxious am I to spare you any annoyance, were it not that it must be referred to in order to show you the real extent of my blame in what has passed."

She inclined her head haughtily, but did not speak. He continued :

"Your father sought my aid to rescue his possessions from escheatment. I rendered him that service, and he desired to requite me. In that desire your family was united ; and I told them that they could make no requital save with your hand. That was readily promised to me, and, indeed, my offer was accepted as in some measure a further advantage to your house, by all save yourself."

" And I gave you reasons which should have satisfied a man of honour."

" They would have satisfied me had they not been answered by the counter reasons of your friends. You will forgive me when I say that the passion you had roused made me perhaps too willing to accept any explanation which would permit me to persevere in my suit."

His iteration of the nature of his esteem for her became unbearable.

"You mean that the purpose you had to serve made you resolute to persevere, indifferent to what sorrow a mere woman might endure."

"Purpose!" he exclaimed, raising his heavy eyebrows, "what purpose could I have other than yourself presented to me? You had no wealth of lands or gold to bring me."

"But my father had kinsmen, had followers whose arms might be of valuable service to you in the crooked paths through which your policy winds to favour."

The clearness of her vision into his motives and the sharpness with which she laid them bare, produced a pause, but he was too well skilled in the command of his countenance to permit it to display the least change.

"I see your prejudice enables you to misconstrue me at every turn. Had I sought only a powerful ally, I think a more powerful one than the Janfarie's might have been found in Scotland—with the hand of a dame more kindly to my deserts."

There was a touch of injured honesty in his manner, but Katherine's repugnance was too keen for her to be deceived by it.

"I am content to wish your choice had been made more in accordance with your merits, sir," she responded; "and so beseech you to proceed with what brevity you may, and release me from this thraldom."

He bit his lips and bowed.

"Your wish, madam, shall be obeyed.

I yielded then to my own desire and the arguments of your family. I became persuaded that your attachment to a ruined and absent gentleman was a girlish fancy which would disappear as soon as you became aware that your parents were bent upon our union."

"Because you would not release them from a hasty promise given in the heat of gratitude."

"Again you misinterpret and compel me to remind you that the marriage was as much desired by those to whom you were bound to render obedience as by myself."

"Say on."

"These were the grounds on which I, unhappily for myself, rejected your appeal, and permitted the matter to go forward. I am still convinced that had not your gay gallant appeared upon our bridal day you would have been content to bear the honours it was in my power to bestow on you as Lady Cochrane."

" You are mistaken, for I had prepared a means of release should I be driven to the last extremity."

" And pray what were the means which were so well concealed from all others ? "

" Death."

" Tush !—that is the merest babble of a silly child. You would have been wiser, credit me."

" I pray that you may never have it in your power to put me to the test."

" I trust that aught I may do will never form so harsh a test of your obduracy, madam, for it can have no better name. Had I known in time my person was so hateful to you I would have held myself in poor esteem if I had prosecuted my cause. Even now I would freely release you were it not that all Scotland knows you as my bride.   To relinquish you now would be to present myself to the world as a coward and a fool—to be laughed and jeered at as a dishonoured man unworthy of the name and title he bears."

Her heart palpitated, for he spoke in a cold hard voice, indicative not only of his resolution but also of his power to enforce it.

"What would you do?" she asked, bending forward with anxious gaze.

"I would first endeavour, for the love I bear you, to persuade you from the mad course on which you have ventured."

"And that failing?"

"Then, madam, I must compel you, for my own reputation's sake, to renounce your present folly, and to go with me to the home I have provided for you.   There I will endeavour to forget your escapade, and will adopt such measures to prevent a repetition of it as your conduct may render necessary."

" You think it is in your power, then, to compel me ? "

" I am sure of it."

Her cheeks were tingling with the mingled sensations of shame and rage.

" And I am as sure that you will fail."

" Sick children and the insane, madam, dread the physician who labours to save them," he retorted, with a cold smile.

" But I am neither a sick child nor an insane woman."

" Then you will be guided by reason, and you will resume something of the discretion you have so far set at defiance. If you be sane you cannot wish to remain longer under the protection of one whose treachery has destroyed your father."

" It is false."

" You wish to believe it so ; but you

cannot surely deny the testimony of your brothers and your kinsmen, Musgrave and Fenwick, however lightly you may value mine."

"It cannot be true," she murmured in a low voice that was like a moan, and pressing her hands on her brow, overcome by the calm assurance with which he made the assertion.

"It is sadly too true," he proceeded, eagerly taking advantage of her distress in the hope that it would help to bring her to submission: "the guilt rests wholly on Lamington's head, and he will speedily have to answer it, and other matters, before the Lords of the Council."

"Ah!" she cried, her face brightening, "he will prove himself blameless."

"It is impossible, unless crime can change its nature. He will be condemned."

"It will be by forsworn judges, then,

and I will know where to find their instigator."

"Would you have your father's assassin escape? Is there no drop of the Janfarie blood in your veins that calls out for vengeance?"

"No; I seek no vengeance. I am content with justice."

"And that you shall have, I swear to you; but you must yourself render justice to others."

"In what, and to whom?"

"To me, whom you have so bitterly wronged, that a whole life's submission would be poor atonement. You owe justice to me, whose head is bowed under the disgrace you have wrought me."

He spoke with an affectation of frankness and injured dignity which was sufficiently effective upon an honourable nature such as hers to make her keenly sensible that the man had suffered some wrong at her hands.

She was abashed and silent.

He saw his advantage, and was not slow to avail himself of it to the uttermost.

"I have explained our position," he continued, in the same strain. "I have told you why I must persist in thrusting upon you a duty which seems so little to your liking, and from which I would therefore gladly release you, but that in doing so I must go and hide my head in some obscure corner of the earth, and forego the brilliant prospect which is almost now within my grasp. Surely, madam, you cannot blame me for my persistence under these circumstances?"

He paused, as if expecting her to speak; but she could not yet. She was too much confused and troubled by the new light in which her conduct appeared to her; and she averted her face to conceal the agitation expressed there.

As he observed this a scarcely perceptible glimmer of triumph crossed his face, and he went on—

" I am aware that I am no dame's chevalier, and that I am perhaps too abstracted —too deeply busied in the great affairs of state ever to make a wooer who will tickle a romantic girl's ear with honeyed mouthings. But I am no goblin either, I trust. There is no deformity in my person, no cloven hoof to shock the eye; and if I cannot make soft speeches, I can at least render you honourable services."

" I do not doubt it, sir; " but——"

" Nay, do not qualify so small an admission. I am prepared to forget what has passed, and I will use what skill I may command to stifle the rumours which have already got afloat to your discredit. I will stand between you and the tongue of scandal; I will win honours for you that shall place you so high that no envious breath shall tarnish your good name. I stand so well in the king's favour, that there is no dignity your heart can crave that I will not obtain for you."

"Enough, sir, enough; these are things to move an ambitious mind, but they cannot change a faithful heart."

But he would not be stayed; he believed she was yielding, and that her protestations were the surest indications of it.

"Already the first earldom of our nobility—the title which stands next to the throne itself—the earldom of Mar, which the king's younger brother bore, is at my disposal. Within a few days it will be mine, and you shall share it. As Countess of Mar you will forget the childish passion which has made you so indiscreet, and in time, Katherine, you will learn to think of me even with some small favour."

Moved by the fervency of his own speech, and misinterpreting her confusion, he approached her and attempted to take her hand. But with a half-smothered cry of alarm she sprang away from him.

"Do not touch me," she cried, breathlessly, her eyes flashing indignation upon him. "All that you have said serves no better purpose than to show me how little you can esteem a woman's nature. Were it in your power to elevate me to the throne itself, so near to which you offer to place me, I would reject your proposal. I have told you that nothing can move me from my resolution to share the good or ill-fortune of him to whom my troth was pledged long ago ; and you, sir, must hold my fidelity at slight value in thinking that you can purchase it with titles that would be to me only the badges of my own falsehood."

His features were for an instant distorted with rage and chagrin; but the next instant his countenance was calm.

" You are determined, then, to force me to my last resource ? "

" I would ask you to pity me, but I see that it would be useless. Do your worst, then, and I will trust to a power greater than any of earth to give me protection."

With his eyes fixed steadily on her, he approached, and in spite of her efforts to avoid him, he grasped her wrist.

" You will not yield to any persuasion," he said, deliberately. " You would still defy the sacred rights that made you mine; you would still link yourself to the man whose hand is red with your father's blood;

and you would leave me to the mockery of the world."

"You hurt me, sir," she said, defiantly, and endeavouring to wrench her arm from him.

"Be calm, madam, and hear me. Since nothing that I have said can influence you to your own benefit, or to justice to me, I must deal with you as the wayward child you are."

"Help, Richard Janfarie—help, brother, help!" she cried, raising her voice, and struggling with all her strength to free herself.

But neither her cries nor her struggles disturbed the implacable resolution of his dark visage.

"You shall be taught submission, mistress, by means of the mad humour which has driven you to such desperation."

She made no other answer, than by con-

tinuing her call for help; and she fancied
that the heavy curtains which screened the
recesses of the central windows were
agitated.

"Be silent and listen," he said, sternly;
"if you have any heed for the safety of
Lamington—but it may be your care for
him is as false—— "

He paused, seeking a simile, and she
filled up the blank.

"It is as true as my contempt for you is
deep."

"You shall prove that. The Abbot is
coming hither presently, to consider the
appeal I have lodged with him for the
arrest of Bertrand Gordon, of Lamington,
and for his authority to support my title to
carry you hence by force."

"No good man will give his authority to
such a project."

"I am content to hazard that, for you

yourself shall weigh the balance down in my favour."

"I?" she gasped, becoming suddenly still, so much was she confounded by this new effrontery. "Your cunning will work marvels indeed if it can make me say aught save that you are no true man in having tortured me thus."

"You are heated, mistress, and I take no count of your words. The Abbot will, most like, ask you to decide whether you will go with me or not."

"And I will tell him that I will only accept the protection of Lamington."

With a malicious glimmer in his eyes, Cochrane brought his face close to hers.

"And at the moment you make that declaration Lamington will be stricken dead at your feet."

She started back with a cry of fear and horror, but he still held her tightly.

"I will denounce your villainous intention."

"No, you will not do that, for it would only hasten his doom. You will see that I am prepared for every emergency."

He dragged her to the first screened window, and he drew the curtain aside.

In the recess two men were standing with swords drawn as if ready to rush forth at a given signal to execute the treacherous design which Cochrane had revealed to the unfortunate lady.

"You know the signal," said Cochrane, as if taking a fiendish delight in showing her how carefully his mine had been laid.

"We do," answered the men, stolidly.

He dropped the curtain, and then drew her to the next window. There also she saw two men with their naked swords glittering in the sunlight. The same question and answer were repeated; and again the curtain covered the hidden executioners.

Cochrane surveyed her dumb consternation with apparent satisfaction. Then, after a pause, to permit her to realize the full terror of her situatiou, he said, slowly:

" Are you satisfied that your resistance cannot help yourself, and will bring destruction upon him ? "

" I am satisfied that you are a demon," she ejaculated, passionately.

" Say rather a man who never allows his resolution to be baulked. They are coming—remember Lamington's life depends upon your word; and the slightest movement of your hand, or the faintest glance of your eye that would betray me, is his death-warrant."

He released her at the moment when the approaching footsteps which had warned him that the Abbot and his company were at hand, halted at the door. Janfarie, who had been on the watch, threw the door open.

The Abbot, David Panther, entered first. He was a tall, stoutly-built man. His features were massive, and of a rather ruddy complexion, as if he were one accustomed to good living, although the gravity of his bearing accorded well with his position, and dispelled any irreverent reflections which a first glance at his face might have inspired.

His eyes were large, and twinkled with an expression that seemed to be composed equally of shrewdness, cunning, and good humour. They were eyes to dance at a good jest without being over particular as to its character, and at the same time they were eyes to penetrate motives, and quick to sum up the real nature of any one who might be brought directly under their observation.

In brief, Panther was a man who could buckle on the armour which his position in those days privileged him to wear, and who could do good service in the field for his own cause; a man who could compete in policy with the cunningest courtier of the period, and who could be royally merry when occasion served, whilst no Churchman could better uphold the dignity of his order.

The Abbot was followed by the Prior, a sharp-featured man, whose body seemed to be worn by the austerities he practised. After him entered Lamington, whose face was singularly pale, and whose eyes moved restlessly round the chamber until they rested upon Katherine. Then they brightened, as if his mind were relieved of some doubt, but he did not approach her.

11

She remained where Cochrane had left
her, on the right hand of the chair of state,
transfixed and bewildered between her
terror of the treachery which threatened
her lover, and her doubt of the consequences to him and to herself, if she should
attempt to save his life by suppressing the
truth. The dilemma was so terrible, and
the necessity to decide one way or the
other so imminent, that she was distracted.
She could neither speak nor move, but
only stand with pallid face bent toward
the floor, striving to collect her sadly
confused thoughts.

The Abbot eyed her curiously as he
passed to the chair of state, and observed
that she made no movement to salute him.
He took his seat without a word, and
the Prior, as next in authority, occupied a
chair on his right. Twelve monks ranged
themselves round their superiors: and

Richard Janfarie, who had entered last, with moody brow and slow step, took his stand near Cochrane. The latter saluted the Abbot with grave courtesy, and, bonnet in hand, stood calmly awaiting the issue of the trial.

CHAPTER X.

THE ABBOT'S COURT.

"Quhat waefou wae her bewtie bred,
    Waefou to young and auld;
Waefou, I trow, to kyth and kin,
    As story ever tauld."

                                        Hardyknute.

A S soon as the Abbot had taken his seat he bowed gravely to Sir Robert Cochrane in recognition. The latter acknowledged his courtesy with less of his usual extreme politeness than he had ever displayed to one at whose hands he expected a service of any kind. Cold and calculating as the man's nature was, Katherine's fair face had obtained some

influence over him that was not altogether
due to his speculations as to the number of
troopers her kinsmen could bring into the
field to support his cause whenever he
might need them.

This influence, strengthened by his
chagrin in being made the fool of such a
trick as that by which Lamington had
carried the bride away, and still more
heightened by her resistance and dislike,
was urging him forward in his course with
a degree of passion which somewhat interfered with the policy that in all other
matters had guided his steps surely to pre-
ferment and success. His was one of those
stubborn minds which only persevere the
more in the attainment of an object as the
difficulties surrounding it increase.

Under these conditions he had been so
far affected by the interview which he had
just held with Katherine that it quickened

to anxiety his desire for the successful issue
of his appeal to the Abbot, and rendered
him fearful of any inopportune discovery
of the ruse by which he hoped to influence
Katherine's decision.　Hence his somewhat
stiff acknowledgment of his lordship's
courtesy.　Slight as was the indication of
his mental disturbance, the Abbot noted it ;
but without making any sign that might
reveal his observation, he proceeded at once
to the business in hand.

"You have made a sudden call upon me,
Sir Robert Cochrane, to a singular duty,"
he said ; "but the emergency will excuse
its abruptness.　Besides, untimely as the
call may be, as you have made it in the
name of the king—a name we all respect
and are bound to serve to the abandonment
of all other claims save only those of
Heaven—I attend here to review the subject of your complaint, and to render you

justice so far as it is within human power to do so. Speak, then, and let us know your wrong, that we may right it if that be possible."

The Abbot's voice was of a deep bass tone, which added to the authority of his presence, and which, in the almost breathless stillness of the audience, sounded upon their ears with peculiar solemnity.

The words reached Katherine where she stood in mute stupefaction, at first as if spoken in the distance, but gradually the sound became more distinct, the meaning penetrated her mind and recalled her to a shuddering sense of all the peril of her position; and filled her at the same time with a sensation of new dread, for she fancied that the Abbot was disposed to favour her persecutor. She listened with wildly throbbing pulse, but she did not raise her head.

Cochrane advanced a pace nearer to the judge by whom he had elected to have his cause tried.

"I crave your lordship's indulgence," he said suavely, and bowing low, "for intruding my pitiful affairs upon you at a time when doubtless you are much occupied with the weighty matters of your holy office. But accident has led me hither, and for that I am thankful, since it has brought me within the hearing of so wise a judge. My cause needs only the impartial review of such an one as your lordship; and indeed it falls within the very palm of your sacred office to do me justice."

"Proceed," rejoined the Abbot, inclining his head slightly. There was a momentary twinkle in his eyes as if he fully appreciated the depth of Cochrane's sincerity in the compliments he offered.

"Yonder lady is the source of my complaint. Briefly, this is the whole matter: —Yesterday by the wish and consent of her parents and kinsfolk she was wedded to me. A holy man from Carlisle performed the ceremony with all due rights. But before night had fallen the lady fled from me and from her father's house with the gallant who stands there so pale before you."

"She fled from bondage that had been forced upon her and that was hateful to her, as you, sir, were well aware," interrupted Lamington, haughtily.

"I charge you, Gordon, be silent," said the Abbot, sternly; "we must hear this matter from him who seems most wronged; and as you shall have unbridled speech when he has done, he too must have his say without check from any here."

Lamington bit his lip, but made no attempt to reply.

Katherine trembled, for the rebuke her
lover had received seemed to indicate still
more clearly the favour with which Cochrane was regarded.

"For this protection I give your lordship
thanks," continued the wily courtier, with
a mock air of humility; "but I need not
try the patience even of an enemy in this
matter. You are already acquainted with
it in some measure from my appeal, which
has moved you to summon us to your
presence here. Wherefore I have only to
repeat those charges on which the justice
of my complaint depends."

"That will suffice."

"This lady, then, being newly bound to
me in bonds of wedlock, fled. Her father
and his kindred pursued her and her
gallant to Dumfries. The town was
alarmed, the burgesses rose, and Lamington
by some base trick deceived them, so that

they set the lawful symbol of the Hot Trod at defiance, and assailed our party. Sir Hugh Janfarie, eager to pacify the rioters, rode into their midst, and whilst seeking to explain our purpose there, he was set upon and treacherously slain, if not by the hand of Lamington, by his connivance; wherein the guilt is as much his as if he had struck the blow."

Katherine with startled eyes gazed at Lamington, and he made a hasty movement as if he would interrupt the speaker; but he was checked by a motion of the Abbot's hand.

"We shut our sorrow in our breasts," Cochrane went on, "and turned sternly to the duty that lay before us. We rode with all haste to the tower of Lamington, and failing there to find any tidings of the fugitives, I, having learned that your lordship was at present here, came to seek

your aid in arresting a traitor, and in
rescuing a foolish lady from her own ruin.
At the gate we learned that fortune had
favoured us, and that in coming to seek
your help we had lighted upon those whom
we pursued."

"Your charge is grave against the man
and woman both," said the Abbot, deliberately; "what proof have you to hold it
good?"

"So please you, here is the lady's
brother, Richard Janfarie, who will con-
firm me. He is now chief of his house;
and next to her husband is the guardian
of the dame, holding all the authority of
his kinship to direct her steps. If that be
not enough to prove my charge good, I
will attest it with my life."

He flung his glove down in front of the
state chair, and Lamington sprang eagerly
forward to pick it up.

But the Abbot, rising quickly, planted his foot upon the glove, and gazed frowningly at the challenged and the challenger.

"Stand back, Gordon; and you, Cochrane, take up your glove again. You have made appeal to me in this matter, and you insult my judgment by challenging its justice before it is spoken. Take up your gage, and hold it for more fitting time and place."

The Abbot gave the command with a dignity and authority that could not be opposed.

Lamington drew back, with lips clenched tightly, indicating the disappointment he felt at losing the opportunity of defending his honour with his sword.

Cochrane, sensible that he had made a false step, endeavoured to retrieve it by obeying the command with a submissive bow.

The Abbot resumed his seat.

"Answer you, Janfarie," he said, "so far as your knowledge goes, has Sir Robert Cochrane spoken truly?"

"He has spoken truth in all that he has said. I own it with shame, for it is my sister who has played the wanton, and it is our father who has fallen in striving to rescue her. I, too, call for justice upon yonder man; and I, too, crave your lordship to deliver the woman into the keeping of her husband."

The Abbot turned to Katherine.

"If it be true, madam, that your father has fallen under Gordon's hand, I cannot think that you would wish to consort with him, however strong may be your reasons for shunning him who seems to have the right to call you wife."

"But he is guiltless, my lord," cried Katherine, stretching out her hands appealingly; "if my father has fallen, Lamington had no share in the ill fortune. I alone merit the blame, for it was my act that led him to his doom."

"Speak, then, and acquaint me by what means, by what temptations you were persuaded, to the rash act which has had such sad results."

Katherine related simply in what manner she had been forced to the altar with Sir Robert Cochrane, despite her plighted troth to Lamington; how, even at the altar, she had refused her consent to the union; and how the priest had been compelled to perform the ceremony, notwithstanding her refusal to make the usual responses. She would have told him, too, how she had resolved to die rather than live the wife of one who had so cruelly taken advantage of his position to force her to the marriage; but all the time she had been speaking her heart had been quivering with the knowledge that the assassins were lying in wait, and that any word she uttered might be the signal for Bertrand's destruction. Therefore she omitted much that she might have said in condonement of her own offence.

The Abbot, however, seemed to pity her unhappy circumstances.

" A marriage so forced," he said, " cannot be prosperous, and it is scarcely lawful. Still you erred, madam, in resisting the authority of your parents ; and in a measure they erred too, in seeking to compel your inclination when it was so much opposed to your wishes in this especial matter ; for it is one in which the child's inclinations should be consulted, seeing that upon it so much of her future welfare is dependent. But most of all, you erred, Cochrane, in taking a wife where you found so little favour. I would have deemed you wiser than to risk the perils of such a bridal."

"I could not know the lady's dislike was so fixed," rejoined Cochrane, placidly; "but as we stand now I must insist upon my claim. Thus far I will yield, however, that you may let her choose between me and the assassin of her father."

Katherine's blood became chilled, and she felt as if her heart ceased beating. She would have made instant appeal to be spared such a test, but the cold glittering eye of Cochrane was upon her and arrested her.

"It is a fair proposal," said his lordship, "but first let Gordon answer to the charge you have made of his part in the death of Janfarie."

"By what mishap the knight has fallen," said Lamington, calmly, "I am ignorant.

Till the foul charge was made against me
I knew nothing of his fate. I have had
little reason to be the friend of Janfarie;
but for this lady's sake I would a thousand
times rather have given my own life,
than that his should have been harmed.
Cochrane makes this charge to serve his
own ends, and Richard Janfarie supports
him in it because his passion blinds him to
the truth."

"You swear that by no direct act of
yours you were a party to the deed?"

"I had no further part in this mishap
than you may account due to me, since it
was in pursuing me he fell. I own it was
by me a cry was raised against Sir Robert
Cochrane, but in doing that I sought no
more than to spread confusion amongst his
party so that we might escape them; and
when the cry was raised, Sir Hugh Janfarie was at the monastery of Grey Friars.

What followed after I do not know, and how far I may be answerable for it I leave your lordship to decide."

"Then I decide against you——"

"We may arrest him, then," cried Cochrane, eagerly, "and bring him for trial before the barons and wardens of the Marches."

Katherine grew sick and faint, for it seemed that she was to be left in the power of the man she dreaded, whilst he was to drag Gordon before a court over which he had so much control as the king's favourite. There could only be one result: he would be doomed.

But the next words of the Abbot thrilled her with hope.

"You are too fast, sir; I have not done. I decide against him in so far as I recognize in him the immediate source of the quarrel in which the knight fell: but as he meditated no harm to Janfarie, we must take into account preceding causes, and they seem to me to justify Lamington's effort to elude your vigilance."

"How, my lord?" exclaimed Cochrane, astounded by this sudden adverse turn of the judgment.

"I mean that as you cannot prove it was his hand which struck the blow, and as I can well believe that he would for the daughter's sake avoid doing such harm to the father, we must attribute Janfarie's fate to the accident of the riot rather than to his premeditation. Wherefore of this charge he stands acquitted."

Katherine with difficulty restrained a cry of joy.

"I protest against this decision," said Cochrane, maintaining a polite bearing despite the wrath he felt; "and I will make appeal to a higher power."

" To whom, sir ? "

" To the barons of the Marches—to the King."

" That will be as you please ; and I would say take the matter straight to the King at once, for I doubt the barons will give you little satisfaction, seeing that it was your name which caused the good folks of Dumfries to forget their respect for the symbol of the Hot Trod."

" Your lordship speaks impartially in this at least," was the suave rejoinder. " I will take the matter straight to the King, and meanwhile I will arrest Gordon."

" Nay, by my faith, sir, that would be carrying your contempt for my decision a little too far. None shall touch him here."

" Who, then, will answer for his appearance ? "

" I myself will answer for it," broke in Lamington. " I pledge my troth to meet the charge whenever and wherever my accusers may appoint."

A cold smile of distrust passed over Cochrane's features.

"I fear we need better surety than that you proffer us."

"Then you must hold my desire to prove your falsehood at slighter value than the passages that have taken place between us might warrant you."

"Be satisfied, Cochrane," said the Abbot, somewhat impatiently, "and let us proceed. If his pledge be not enough for you, take mine also."

"I cannot further object, my lord; your word would suffice for a troop of malefactors."

"Your compliments smell something of satire; sauce may be at times too highly flavoured."

"The sincerity of my respect must plead

my excuse for the high seasoning of my
words," was the answer, with the ease of
one accustomed to turn even a rebuke into
a means of flattery.

His lordship, without affecting to observe
the remark, proceeded :

"Your claim to the lady has now to be
disposed of; and that might have been a
more troublesome question to settle than
the other, had not your own generosity
provided a ready way out of the difficulty.
You, madam, shall decide the claims of
your suitors."

"Again I crave your lordship's indulgence," interrupted Cochrane; "my claim
is that of a husband."

"Give it what title you will, sir. But
before she answers, this lady must understand that I, holding important office in
the Church, do not regard as binding the
ceremony through which she seems to

have been dragged, and which was performed by a man who forgot the sanctity
of his order in the terror of his life.   If
she decide against you I will not hesitate
to declare your marriage void, feeling
assured that his holiness the Pope will
sanction my decision."

Cochrane inclined his head slightly to
hide the angry flush which rose to his
countenance, and which for once he was
unable to control.   The proceedings had
opened so much in his favour that he had
counted upon an easy victory : but now
the favour seemed to have so completely
changed sides that he deemed the judge
more than partial to his rival.   As, however, he had provided for the decision in
the event of its being left to Katherine,
according to his apparently frank proposal,
he was content to abide the result, watching her narrowly the while.

CHAPTER XI.

BETWEEN TWO FIRES.

"But fare ye weel, my ae fause love,
   That I hae looed sae lang;
If sets ye chuse another love
   And let young Benjie gaug.

"Then Marjorie turned her round about,
   The tear blinding her e'e—
I darena, darena let thee in,
   But I'll come down to thee."
               Young Benjie.

THE test which she had feared so much had come at last. There was no loop-hole of escape from it—she must either suppress the words she was yearning to speak or hazard Gordon's life. If she had only had any means to warn him ; if she had only had the least chance of putting him on his guard against the sudden assault which she knew would be made upon him, and under which he must fall before he had time to place his hand upon his sword—if the least opportunity to shield him had offered itself, she would have spoken outright, and declared how much she hated Cochrane, whilst she denounced his treachery.

But she saw no outlet of this kind from her pitiable position ; she must leave Lamington to mistrust her, or she must sacrifice him. She had no other alternative. She felt the gaze of Cochrane fixed upon her ; she knew that he understood the struggle of her mind, and that at the least symptom of her intention to defy him, he would give the fatal signal.

" Come, madam, the matter lies in your hands now," said the Abbot, after a pause,

as if he had been waiting for her to speak;
"you have heard my verdict as to the bond
by which Sir Robert Cochrane claims you
as his; but I charge you think well before
you speak, for remember that the wishes
of your parents demand as deep and earnest
consideration from you as your inclination
in this affair should have received from
them. Say, then, do you persist in your
determination, and will you go hence with
Lamington?"

She stood mute and motionless, as if she
had not heard, but the cruel anguish of the
moment was to her more excruciating than
if all she had hitherto endured had been
concentrated in one bitter blow, and it had
fallen now. Her eyes were fixed in terror
upon Cochrane, and he stood implacable as
fate, confident of victory.

She seemed like one suddenly trans-
formed to stone, and was incapable of

speech or motion. But she was painfully
sensible of all that was passing around her.
She felt that Lamington was gazing upon
her, marvelling at her silence. She knew
that the Abbot was eyeing her in astonishment, and that all were wondering at her
strange manner. Yet she could not break
the spell of terror that transfixed her.

"We wait your answer, madam," said
the Abbot, encouragingly, thinking that
some modest fear constrained her, "and
you may give it freely, for here you are
under the protection of the Church."

Still she was silent, and indeed she
scarcely heard the words.

"Katherine!" exclaimed Lamington,
vague doubts beginning to mingle with his
wonder, and affrighting him, "why do you
not speak? Is the question so hard to
answer?—nay, you can have but one
answer, since you have braved the wrath

of kindred and the scorn of unthinking minds for your love's sake. You cannot hesitate to tell them that you will go with me, and with me only."

She made no response yet.

The silence which ensued was like that in which people listen for the last breath of one dying. None but Cochrane and the woman herself knew the meaning of her pause.

The Abbot observed upon whom her eyes were fixed; and authoritatively :

" You seem to be in fear, but you have no cause. I gave Cochrane liberty to speak with you, as he urgently desired, before the court was held; but if he has taken advantage of my license to practise upon you by any undue threat to compel your will, he shall find that I have power to protect you in spite of all his art—ay, in spite of the king himself."

The calm dignity of his speech affected her, and she trembled visibly; but still, bewildered by contending emotions and alarmed by the results which depended on her words, whatever they might be, she could not reply.

With mock humility and apparent anxiety to clear himself of all suspicion, Cochrane spoke:

"I beseech your lordship, give the lady time. I own that I have warned her of certain issues which depend on her, but I will abide by her decision."

The latter words were uttered with a significance that only Katherine comprehended.

The Abbot rose to his feet.

"You have heard what he has said, madam; I charge you, therefore, answer without more delay—go you with Cochrane, as your kinsfolk would have you, or go you with Lamington, as you seemed inclined?"

She made a hasty movement, and her face flushed as if she were determined at all hazards to declare the true sentiment of her heart; but at the same moment Cochrane bent forward, raising his hand slightly. His change of posture seemed to all except Katherine merely indicative of his anxiety about her determination; but to her it signified that he was ready to call the hidden assassins to their foul work.

The impulse to which she had been about to yield was arrested, her heart seemed to be clasped by a hand of ice, and a moment longer she stood quivering and bewildered. Then wildly she flung herself at the feet of the Abbot, and raising her pallid face she cried in piteous agony:

"My lord, my lord, I cannot go with Lamington."

Then she bowed her head to the ground as if to hide her shame and anguish.

There was a moment of speechless wonder, during which Cochrane resumed his ordinary position—a smile of satisfaction on his countenance. Lamington was like one stunned by the unexpected nature of her response. Perplexed as he had been by her hesitation, he had not been at all prepared for this blank rejection of his suit. Wholly unsuspicious of the real motive which inspired her words, he was unable to divine the meaning of the sudden change in her regard for him.

"Is this final, madam?" said the Abbot, much amazed that she should revoke her preference for the man with whom she had taken flight.

His voice roused Gordon.

"Katherine," he cried with passionate vehemence, "you do not know what you have said—you have rejected me, Bertrand! Look up, look up, Katherine, and say that we have misunderstood you—say that our ears have been deceived; say that it was not my name you meant to pronounce."

He had sprung to her side, he bent over her, with the great love he bore her shaking his frame, and making his voice tremble, conjuring her to recall her words.

But she did not raise her head. Trembling with the violent emotions which were torturing her, and sustaining herself with the mental exclamation—"It is for his sake"—she answered him in a voice half stifled by her sobs :

"I cannot go with you."

"Oh, this is some frenzy which has seized her," he ejaculated wildly; "or I have been so basely maligned that she has learned to hate me. If that be so " (raising himself and fiercely confronting Cochrane),

13

" look you, sir, well to your affairs, for you shall not live to enjoy the triumph you have so treacherously won ! "

" We agreed to abide by the lady's decision," was Cochrane's complacent response.

" It has been forced from her by some accursed trick. I will not believe that she could be of so fickle humour as to turn from me now. Katherine ! Katherine ! rise and make known to us by what base means these falsehoods have been wrung from you—for they are false—as false to your own heart as they are false to me."

Low heart-burning sobs were the only response to his passionate appeal.

He staggered back, his eyes starting in their sockets, his hands clenched desperately. There was no sound in the chamber save her stifled murmurs of distress, but in his ears there was a din as of a thousand fiends shouting in mockery the answer she had given—"I cannot go with you!"

Confused by these weird sounds, dazed by the sudden shock he had received, he could not yet believe that she intended to forsake him. He could find no clue to her sudden change. He could have understood it had she believed him to be the guilty cause of her father's death. But she did not credit that; her own lips had declared him as innocent of it in fact as he had been in thought. It could not be either that she had not cared for him, for she had given him too great a proof of her regard.

What, then, could be the meaning of her rejection?

It remained for Cochrane with his oily, venomous tongue to suggest a cause as base as he knew it to be untrue.

"I beseech your lordship," he said with

an anxiety which was not altogether
assumed, " let me remove the lady. You
see how she is afflicted by this interview.
She risked much for this man's sake, knowing too little of his circumstances, and now
that she knows him to be a bankrupt ad-
venturer, she would spare him and herself
the misery which must result from adding
another burden to his beggarly estate."

Katherine did not hear his words; her
distress deafened her to the calumny which
was being spoken.

Lamington heard, and a thrill of pain
quivered in his breast and overwhelmed his
dismay in scorn for the mind which could
at such a moment make such sordid calcu-
lations. He had been striving vainly for
some explanation of her conduct, and in his
blind passion he accepted the first that
offered itself.

" Merciful powers!" he exclaimed,

gazing upon her, doubt mingled with his despair, " can this be so ? Is this why she hides her head from me, and cannot raise her face to mine ? Speak, woman ; if your fair looks have not cheated me with the thought that you had as fair a heart—let me know if this knave has spoken truly, so that I may turn from you so full of scorn, that I shall feel no pang for all the hopes and love you have trampled under-foot ! "

" It is for his sake that I am silent," she again murmured to herself, and still she gave him no reply.

With a species of frenzy he stooped down and seized her arm.

" Have you lost all sense of hearing and of touch ? or is this no more than another trick to feign a distress that is a mockery to me ? Oh, madam, if these be your reasons for your new humour, you might

have spared us all much trouble had you
declared them sooner. I am not so poor
but I can thank Heaven for rescuing me
from the false smiles of one who balances
her affection with the stock of a larder or
the stuff of a gown. I deemed you worthy
to share with me the honourable struggle
to win back the name and fortune of my
father's house—I find you now a weak,
pitiful creature, unfit to bear a true gentleman's name."

Katherine suddenly clasped the Abbot's
knees, and looking up to him imploringly,
with tearful face, but not daring to glance
towards her lover, she cried :

"Spare me, my lord, spare me, and take
him away."

Lamington laughed bitterly as he drew
back.

"Oh, be content, madam ; I will relieve
you of my presence without his lordship's

interference. There is your treasure, Cochrane; take her and be as proud of her as you may. By my faith, I thank you for having rescued me from the shame I sought so eagerly; for sad shame it would have been indeed to have found her later what I know her to be now."

"Let me take her hence," said Cochrane again to his lordship; "this madman's raving is unfit for her ears."

"She has heard the last of it," cried Lamington, with the cruel laugh of despair that pierced her to the quick, more on account of his suffering than of her own, great as that was. He went on: "She need never heed me, for I will be the first to congratulate her, and wish her all the joy that she deserves."

"Peace, man," interrupted the Abbot, who had been watching this strange scene with curious eyes, and who began to suspect that Katherine had some deeper reason for her conduct than appeared on the surface. " Peace, and retire."

" Since your lordship commands it, I obey; but it was not needed. Trust me, I would have seen you join the hands of this brave couple with as fair a laugh on my lips as you could have wished. Since they would have me gone, I will humour them in this as in all other things. Fare you well, Mistress Katherine—or Lady Cochrane, I ought to say, although the name sticks in my throat. Farewell, and when you think of me "—here his affected tone of raillery broke down, and his passionate agony found expression—" oh, woman, think of me as of one whose life you have marred—of one who cherished your image above all else on earth—of one whom your falsehood has hurled down the black depths of misery and despair; and yet of one who thanks Heaven that he knows your baseness even while he falls."

"Spare me—spare him," moaned Katherine to the Abbot.

The latter motioned to the Prior, who rose hastily from his seat, and prevented Lamington saying more by dragging him from the chamber.

The door had scarcely closed upon them when the Abbot proceeded :

"I presume, madam, from your rejection of Lamington that you accept the proffered protection of Sir Robert Cochrane ? "

"Undoubtedly that is her meaning," said Cochrane, advancing lightly to raise her from her kneeling posture.

But with a cry of dismay and horror she shrank from his touch, and clung desperately to the knees of the Abbot.

"No, no, my lord, keep him away—his touch would kill me. I throw myself on your mercy—I implore your protection, and I will accept none other."

"In good faith, madam," ejaculated his lordship, a little impatiently, "your conduct is somewhat of the strangest. Explain to me; what does it mean?"

"Her brain is crazed," said Cochrane, hastily; "she does not know her own mind; she will be cured in time, *but the danger is not over yet.*"

The latter words were spoken with a significance which Katherine understood too well. Her impulse had been to answer the Abbot by denouncing Cochrane's treacherous trick, but his warning checked her. She felt that until she had an opportunity to make Lamington aware of the position it would be madness to imperil his life anew by declaring the truth after she had sacrificed so much to save him.

"Be merciful, my lord, and give me your protection," was all she dared to say.

"But I demand your lordship's recognition of her husband's authority by yielding her up to me. Nay, more; here stands her brother, the head of her house, and I demand that you recognize the authority of her family beside my own."

"Rise, lady," said the Abbot, slowly, and assisting her to her feet. "You shall have my protection, since you claim it so earnestly."

She hung, trembling, on his arm, and watching Cochrane's dark visage suspiciously.

"Surely your lordship cannot deny my claims upon her after all that has passed," he said with some uneasiness.

"I deny nothing, Cochrane; but until the lady has had time to recover from the excitement of this trial she shall remain under my charge."

"Then your lordship compels me to warn you that you exceed the powers of your position. You have no right to hold her back from those who are her guardians by law and nature."

"It is my privilege, sir, to protect the weak. You have yourself said that her mind is unbalanced: until she find the balance again I will care for her."

"And I deny your right to do so."

"Your denial is of small account to me; but since your objection is made so strongly, I will place her under the charge of one to whom you cannot object."

"Then you will carry her straight to Lady Janfarie."

"No, I will carry her to the Queen; and whilst she is under her Majesty's protection, you will have opportunity to move her mind to your favour if that be possible. Meanwhile, you may ride with us and see that I discharge my duty faithfully. Come, madam, I will conduct you to a chamber where you may prepare for our journey."

Cochrane, gnawing his lip, but bowing with affected submission, drew back as the Abbot led Katherine from the apartment.

CHAPTER XII.

SNARES.

"Here maun I lye, here maun I die,
By treachery's false gyles;
Witless I was that faith e're gave
To wicked woman's smiles."

Hardyknute.

ON the way to the apartment which she had occupied during the night, Katherine felt herself too much depressed and confused to be able to speak. She had warded off the danger which had threatened the life of him to whom her whole heart was devoted; but she had done it at the cost of excruciating torture to herself and to him, and the exhaustion which ensued naturally left her weak and sick. Besides, there was the bitter consciousness that, notwithstanding all she had suffered and risked, the safety it had secured was only temporary.

She now knew to what cruel extremities Cochrane was prepared to proceed in order to possess her, and to redeem the discredit which her flight had thrown upon him; and she dreaded the power his cunning and position afforded him to carry his determination into effect.

Indeed, she had been so much impressed by the peril that must be encountered in braving such a man as Cochrane, that even when she had reached her room, and the Abbot was about to leave her, she hesitated whether or not it would be well to hazard what might happen on her acquainting him with the trick by which she had been controlled, and which had rendered her conduct so singular and inconsistent.

"Here you will rest, daughter," said his lordship, kindly, and dropping into the paternal form of address befitting his character of a Church dignitary; "and I will see that refreshment is provided for you. You will be free from interruption till I send for you, and by that time you may have recovered the calmness of mind which has been so much disturbed."

Still hesitating whether to reveal her secret now or to delay until she found more fitting opportunity, she bowed her head and spoke falteringly:

"My words are feeble, good father, and cannot make known to you as I would wish the gratitude I feel."

"Gratitude is always deepest, child, when it is voiceless. But why have you sought my protection since, having rejected that of Lamington, it would seem more natural for you to have accepted Cochrane's or your brother's guardianship?"

She glanced around her in a quick, affrighted manner, and spoke in a whisper.

" Where is he now ? "

" You mean Lamington ?—he is in the private chamber of the Prior, waiting for me. Why do you look about so strangely? No harm can reach you here."

" Who can tell that?" she sighed bitterly. "Last night I thought that within this holy house we were safe, but this morning I have learned that even here treachery and the hand of the assassin can reach us."

" Your manner and your words are so strange, daughter," said the Abbot, slowly, and with a passing doubt that her mind had become slightly crazed, " that I am perplexed exceedingly. Life is at best

14

uncertain, but in this house it should be safe at least from the dangers you point at."

"But it is not so. Oh, good father, you saw the anguish I endured whilst refusing the man I had made choice of in despite of all my kindred. You saw the horror with which the touch of Cochrane thrilled me, and you could not understand the contradiction of my words and looks. But you shall know my reason now, if I may speak in assurance that no ears save yours can hear my words."

The Abbot, wondering, walked to the door, looked along the passage, and saw that it was clear. Then he returned to Katherine.

"Speak, daughter, and have no fear. I pitied your distress when your conduct was a riddle to me; be sure that you will have all the aid it is in my power to give, when I have learned the motives which have prompted your behaviour."

Rapidy she related to him the manner in which Cochrane had threatened her, and compelled her to deny the impulse of her heart in refusing to accompany Lamington when the matter seemed to be left entirely to her option.

The Abbot, as he listened, was first surprised by the boldness of the trick which Cochrane had played them, and next indignant.

" I understand you now, daughter, and I may tell you I divined that you had some hidden motive for your conduct. I was blind not to have seen at once that there was knavery at the back of it, knowing Cochrane as I do. His affected generosity should have betrayed him to me at once, for there is no kindly spark in his whole nature for other than his wretched self.

But he shall answer for every pang he has caused to you."

" I implore you, good father, do not let him know yet that I have revealed his treachery; and give Bertrand instant warning, for this man has power and is remorseless."

" Keep a light heart, child, on that score. We have hunted foxes before now, and it shall go hard but our experience will outwit this one."

" Thanks, thanks, father. Keep Bertrand safe, and you will find me wanting neither in courage nor patience."

" I will bear your message to him, and will contrive that you shall see him, so that he may learn your truth from your own lips."

" He will not blame me when he knows all ?" she said, with timid doubt.

" He shall not—rest you satisfied.

Meanwhile bar your door, and keep all out whose company may not be agreeable to you."

Therewith he pronounced a paternal benediction and withdrew. Katherine immediately followed his directions and barred the door, for she feared, and with some reason, that, disappointed in the decision of the Abbot's court, Cochrane might seek her, either to persuade her to remain silent as to his knavery, or to force her away with him, notwithstanding his apparent submission to his lordship's authority.

The Abbot Panther, pondering upon what he had just heard, and upon other matters with which it was more or less associated, made his way along various corridors to the private chambers of the Prior.

He entered a species of ante-room, at the

farther end of which was a small door covered by heavy hangings. Through this doorway he passed into a square apartment which was furnished with some degree of comfort.

There he saw Lamington, with flushed face and excited manner, pacing the floor; whilst the Prior, who had apparently exhausted all the persuasion at his command, sat gravely silent watching him.

On the entrance of the Abbot, the Prior rose, and in obedience to a whisper, noiselessly retired to the ante-room, where he remained, evidently for the purpose of insuring the safety of his superior from any interruption or eavesdroppers.

Lamington halted abruptly.

" Well, is she gone ? " he queried, with quivering lips, although he tried to speak lightly.

" Gone!—no, nor does she mean to go except under my care."

Lamington glowered at him, unable to comprehend the answer.

"What new whim is this?" he said, bitterly. "Has her fickle brain already repented the wrong she has done me?"

"She has done you a service, not a wrong. We are blind creatures, all of us, and do not see the good which comes to us often in the form of affliction."

"You count it a service, then, for her to have renounced me?"

"Under the circumstances it was so. Come, sit down and listen to me. You shall learn that Mistress Katherine was most kind when she seemed most cruel."

Lamington drew back with an exclamation of pain.

"I will not listen to you or any man who comes to tell me that she has not been fooling me. Fair opportunity was given her to decide between the man from whom she had fled and myself. She has made her choice, and so let her abide by it. For me, I will not seek to compel any woman's humour, although I suffered all the tortures the arch-fiend could invent by the loss of her."

"You are too hot, my son," said the Abbot, quietly; "the lady had no choice save to appear fickle to you or to sacrifice your life."

"Am I then so poor a wretch that she feared my capability to defend myself against a knave like Cochrane? That is the sharpest sting of all."

"Be calm, man, and listen. In a fair and open struggle no one, and she least of all, would doubt your prowess. But the strongest is weak against a secret foe."

"Cochrane makes no secret of his enmity."

" But he hides the means wherewith he seeks to strike at you."

" Let him do his worst."

" Ay, let him do it; but let us be prepared to meet it. Sit down, I say; and when you have heard her explanation, if you do not pity her, and take prompt measures on your own, and her behalf, you cannot care so much for the lady as you seem to do."

With an impatient gesture, as if to intimate how little satisfaction he expected from the explanation, Lamington at length seated himself opposite his friend. The Abbot had laid aside his mitre and surplice, and with the removal of these insignia of his office, his manner seemed to change insensibly. He spoke now without any of that dignified composure which had characterized his speech while he had been holding the court. His words were uttered with a quick and sharp enunciation, and his observations were those of a man experienced in worldly ways, and of one whose mind was occupied with many schemes. In fact, the Churchman had disappeared and the politician had taken his place.

Astounded by the revelation which was made to him, Lamington sat for a moment breathless; then starting to his feet with hands clenched, he moved towards the door.

"By every saint in heaven he shall answer for this treachery before he is many minutes older. Shame upon me to have blamed her as I have done—to have heaped my mad maledictions upon her while she was trying to save me."

His hand was on the door.

"Come back, come back, hot-brained and short-sighted mortal. I expected that this intelligence would move you to pity for her and shame for yourself; but, my faith, I did not expect you to act so blindly."

"How, blindly? Would you persuade me to forego my vengeance or to pause in it?"

"Nay, I would not have you forego it; but I would have you pause that it may be the more complete."

"Show me how that may be done—show me how I can whip his heartless nature into some part of the agony she has endured, and I will wait for years. But be sure that you give him no chance to escape me, or I will hold you my enemy."

"We shall not have to wait long, I trust, to bring the knave to account, and you shall see that the course you were about to take just now would be the clearest way to give him the chance of escape which you fear he may obtain."

" Read the riddle to me. I listen with what patience I have left."

" Come nearer, then."

Lamington approached slowly, as if he were still doubtful whether or not his best course was to seek Cochrane at once.

The Abbot, with a pawky smile, proceeded :

" I have already told you something of the purpose for which I trysted you to meet me here. Now, in all these unexpected events which have transpired, I see a direct means of assisting our project and of satisfying your desire for retribution."

" You will work a marvel indeed if you can turn these miseries to so good account."

" You will see. First, you know the power which this knave Cochrane and his fellows have obtained over the King. They have played upon his Majesty's weakness and upon his good nature, to the ruin of all honest men, and the degradation of our country."

" All that I know—a set of mountebanks govern the State and make us bow our heads in helpless wrath."

" They must be removed; and the chief of them must suffer first. His Majesty's brothers, the Duke of Albany and the Earl of Mar, have determined upon this as much for their brother's sake as for their own. They have the support of every noble who still attends the court, besides the devoted services of the many who have been banished and deprived of titles and lands by the influence of this Cochrane. The people are groaning under his oppression, and you yourself have proved at Dumfries with what good will they would rise to expel the tyrant."

" But how can the treachery which has

tortured Katherine and distracted me help forward this purpose ?"

" In this way : I am to place Mistress Katherine under the Queen's protection. She will tell her Majesty the story of the persecution with which Cochrane has assailed her, and of the villainy by which he attempted to force her to submission."

" But he will deny it all when he is charged with it."

" Ay, but trust me, Margaret of Denmark is a lady of as clear vision as of warm sympathy. She will be interested in Mistress Katherine's misfortunes, and she will recognize her truth, no matter what Cochrane may say to the contrary."

" But the King will not believe so readily."

" Well, then, it is a question of the Queen's influence upon his Majesty opposed

to that of Cochrane; and if she take up
the matter in the earnest spirit which I
calculate upon, then I will weigh a wife's
skill against the cajolery of a hundred
favourites."

" And if it fail ?"

At the question the Abbot leaned back
on his chair, folding his hands complacently
before him and smiling incredulously.

" If it fail," he answered, in a low,
cautious tone, " if the Queen does not
depose an unworthy favourite, then I am
afraid that the King himself will pay the
penalty of his obstinate fidelity to the
harpies who surround him."

" And that penalty ? "

" Will be his crown."

Lamington started and drew back.

" How say you ?—this is treason of the
boldest flight."

" It is justice to the people and to the

King himself, only you choose to give it an
unpleasant name. We have no intent to
disturb lawful authority, but we are resolved
that the greedy cormorants who surround
the throne, sapping its honour, and making
it a thing of contempt for the world, shall
be driven thence. The cry of wrong-
doing swells on every side, and it has
grown too loud ever to be hushed until
the cause of it is removed. His Majesty's
own safety demands that the parasites
who are battening on his weakness shall
be removed, and the outcry of the people
commands it."

"But let them be removed without
danger to the King."

"So much we hope to do; but even
kings must take physic sometimes."

"I will have no hand in aught that
threatens the safety of our sovereign," said
Gordon, resolutely.

"Why, who is there makes such a threat? Albany and Mar are his brothers, and they seek only to insure his safety which his own folly has so far imperilled that a breath would rouse the country to arms against him."

"Pledge me your word that there is no other object, and I am with you."

"Most faithfully I pledge myself; for, as I understand the matter, we seek to serve the King, not to harm him. Surely, you have little reason to be dainty about the means by which Cochrane and his fellows may be swept from the height which gives them power to ruin honest men."

That reminder of his own wrongs stirred anew the passion of Lamington, which had been for a moment chilled by the boldness of the conspiracy now revealed to him.

"There is my hand," he responded,

impulsively. "You shall not find it falter until justice shall have wrought its work upon Robert Cochrane."

The Abbot grasped his hand tightly.

"Your word is pledged," he said, hastily, his eyes glistening with satisfaction, "and the misery Katherine has endured should hold you to it steadily. For her sake I trust you to be discreet and watchful."

"Name her when you see me hesitate, and the memory of her suffering will make me remorseless."

"Remember, then, that she is the prize for which you struggle; and remember, too, that justice must be done to your father's name."

"Ay, these are motives to fit a man for desperate deeds."

"Enough, then; our course is clear. It was to explain these things to you that I

wished you to meet me at this place. Now
go see the lady, and make what amends to
her you can for the blame you unjustly
cast upon her. Poor dame! your wild
charges hurt her more than all the rest."

"I will make atonement, if it be in the
power of man to expiate such wrong, by
the faithful service of a life. Heaven knows
I, too, suffered something. But I will
explain that to her," he continued, with
an attempt to shake off the depression
which had weighed upon him since that
stormy meeting; "and you, most reverend
father, when you have donned your canoni-
cals again and forgotten that you are a
courtier—ay, and one of the cunningest,
too—you will see that the ceremony which
was performed at Johnstone is declared
null."

The Abbot gave a quiet but jovial sort
of laugh at the reference to his double

character. As has been seen, when performing any of the duties appertaining to his position as a Church dignitary, he acted with a solemnity that inspired respect; but with his badge of office he laid aside the churchman, and in his second character he schemed and intrigued with an address which earned for him a high place in the estimation of the courts of England, France, and of his own country. He made little attempt to conceal these contradictory traits of his nature, and he could enjoy a joke at his own expense with any man. In this respect, at least, he was no hypocrite, although he was by no means particular as to the stratagem by which he might outwit an opponent.

"Away you to the dame," he said, still laughing, "and if it will comfort her, say that the ceremony shall be annulled before three days have passed. But bid her beware lest by any look or sign she should permit Cochrane to know that we have discovered his treachery before we have reached Linlithgow. Till then you must bid her adieu, for you must not speak to her again during the journey. Go; the Prior will show you her chamber."

Lamington, with a light step and a relieved heart, hastened to seek Katherine; and he had no presentiment of the dire events that were to bar their meeting.

CHAPTER XIII.

THROUGH THE WOOD.

> "' I lo'e Brown Adam, weel,' she said,
> ' I trow sae does he me;
> I wad nae gie Brown Adam's love
> For nae fause knight I see.'"
>
> *Brown Adam.*

KATHERINE remained half an hour undisturbed in her apartment after the Abbot had quitted her. She experienced an immeasurable sense of relief now that she had unburthened her mind of the wretched secret by which her actions had been controlled, and by which she had been made to appear so fickle in the eyes of the man whose esteem she valued most.

Every moment she expected to hear Lamington knock and demand admission. Her mind became concentrated upon that expectation, and her sense of hearing was strained to catch the sound of his approaching footsteps.

At length, a light tap on the door.

She sprang toward it with a subdued cry of joy.

"Who is there?" she asked, with her hand trembling on the bar, ready to withdraw it.

"Open, sister; I bear a message to you," was the answer, in a low voice.

She was disappointed and chagrined; for an instant she even felt a shaft of spleen at the laggardliness of her lover. He should have been as eager as herself, she thought, for the reconciliation which was to atone for the affliction they had both undergone. Reflection, however, soothed her, for doubtless he had sent this message to announce his approach.

" A message from whom ? "

" From one, sister, who waits eagerly your presence and forgiveness."

She opened the door.

A friar, with bowed shoulders and cowl drawn closely over his head, concealing his features, which were still further hidden by his eyes being sedulously bent upon the ground, stood on the threshold.

" Is he coming ? " she questioned eagerly.

" Nay, sister," was the answer, in a still lower tone than before, and with an oddly guttural utterance. " You are to follow me, and join him. I have no knowledge of his reasons for this strange conduct; but he told me that you would understand when I said that it was needful for your safety and for his that you should pass hence unseen."

"Said he so? I will go with you instantly."

And without pausing to speculate upon the motives which could have prompted this sudden flight after the Abbot had promised his protection, she hastily snatched up the plaid her lover had placed round her on the previous night, threw it round her shoulders, drawing it over her head, and followed the friar.

He had turned his back on her the moment he had observed she was prepared to accompany him. When she whispered, "I am ready," he moved noiselessly along the passage.

At the top of the staircase he half turned his face toward her.

"Step quickly, sister," he said under his breath, "and lightly, for we must pass the chamber of one whose eyes we are to avoid."

Holding her breath, she descended the stairs after him with the lightness and rapidity of a fawn. When they entered the second passage from which the one leading to the royal apartments diverged, she trembled lest Cochrane or her brother should break out upon them and bar their progress.

But although she heard footsteps in various directions, no one crossed their path. Uninterrupted they reached a small side door, which her guide opened quickly, and they passed out to the garden square of the Priory.

In this square the monks of the establishment at stated hours took exercise, walked and meditated upon the affairs of the small world to which their devotion limited them, and upon the great future for which they were preparing themselves. Round the walls were niches and seats for the promenaders to rest when they were so disposed. Above the niches were carved images of saints and allegories of good and evil, to help the thoughts of the holy men when they were tempted to stray from the high purpose of their devotions.

As it wanted yet an hour to the time of the forenoon promenade, the square was unoccupied, else the appearance of a woman in the garb of the world in that place would have attracted attention and excited curious questioning probably from some of the brotherhood.

Evidently afraid lest anything of this kind might happen, and lest his character might be affected by discovery, Katherine's guide said hurriedly—again only partly turning his face toward her—

" Hasten, good sister, and keep close to the wall, as you observe me do."

" I will keep pace with you, make what speed you will."

" Once outside the square, and we are safe."

" We ? "

His shoulders jerked as if he had stumbled.

" Ay, we," he added quickly, but without looking round at all, " for I risk something, sister, in serving you and your friend."

"I understand, father, and I am grateful."

Keeping close to the wall which ran on a line with the main wall of the house, so that they could not be seen unless some one thrust his head out of a window, they at a pace accelerated almost to a run, made for the end of the square. They reached it, still apparently undiscovered.

A small oaken door, studded with massive iron bolts, was opened by the friar with a key which he held ready in his hand.

They passed through the doorway and stood on the outside of the Priory.

Katherine looked round : the black forest was looming before her, its trees waving and sighing in the wind, and down below, the Ken was glistening in the sunlight as it rippled slowly through the dell.

But Lamington was not there, and she turned with some disappointment to her guide.

He was relocking the door, and when he had done so, he threw the key over the wall into the square, as if he had no intention of returning.

That seemed curious ; but she was too anxious to learn why Lamington was not waiting there for her, as she had been led to expect, to give immediate attention to the circumstance.

"Why is he not here?" she queried, wonderingly.

"There was too much danger of being observed for him to tarry here."

"Where is he, then?"

"He is on before us. I will guide you safely to him, do not doubt."

There seemed to be, or her fancy betrayed her, a shade of impatience in the friar's manner, and she almost started at the tone, for it was abrupt, and struck some chord of her memory that roused vague and perplexing suggestions that the voice was not unfamiliar to her, although she could not associate it with any person.

He began to move rapidly across the open space which lay between them and the forest.

Katherine followed, keeping close behind him. Before they had made many paces she spoke again.

"At what place has he appointed to wait for me, father?" she said with some little trepidation, for she feared that her repeated questions annoyed her guide.

"He rides on before, and we are to overtake him," he replied in a more modulated tone than that he had last used.

"Then you go with me?"

"Yes, till I have placed you under his charge. That was my promise. If you doubt me, we will return."

"No, no; I beseech you go on, and pardon my anxiety. But it seems strange that he should desire to depart in this secret fashion when the good Abbot pledged himself to guard us until he had placed me under the care of the Queen."

"His lordship's intention was sincere, no doubt; but you should know that, with all his power, he could not insure you the safety which you and your friend need."

"I have had bitter reason to know that too well, but I thought that when aware of Cochrane's treachery he could take means to thwart him for the present."

"Such a man as Cochrane is not easily thwarted. It is the Abbot's wish that you should reach the Queen as speedily as possible, and the course you are taking seemed the surest and swiftest."

"Did he indeed think so? Ah, then Cochrane's power must be great indeed when even the good Lord Abbot must stoop to such means as this to overreach him."

"His power is great; but pause or go forward as it may suit your pleasure. Only decide now, for in a little while return will be impossible without exposure of the whole stratagem."

"Hasten on; I will not pause again."

By this time they had entered the forest at a point where three footpaths joined.

There the friar hesitated an instant, as if he were not well acquainted with the route, and as if he were not sure which path to take.

At length, with a half-smothered ejaculation of discontent, apparently at his own indecision, he chose the path to the right. That led them along the skirt of the wood in the direction of the Ken.

Katherine's guide evidently did not mean to penetrate the forest. He had rather accepted the shelter of the trees to hide them from observation. This object became clear when, after half an hour's brisk walking, and they had descended into the vale, he suddenly diverged towards an open plain which dipped down to the bank of the river.

Katherine was again wondering how far they would have to go before they overtook Lamington. The recent conversation

16

had satisfied her for the time; but as they progressed without discovering any trace of her lover, she was beginning again to feel surprised that he should have left her to traverse such a distance under the guidance of any one save himself. She did not like to express this feeling, because already the guide had been displeased by her anxiety, which seemed so like doubt of his fidelity.

They were within a few paces of the glade when the friar halted and bowed his head towards the ground, as if listening.

She watched him anxiously, and she too listened. In the distance a faint halloo was heard, and as the sound was repeated it seemed to grow louder and nearer, as if approaching them.

"Your absence is discovered," said the friar, in a quick undertone. "We are pursued. Speed now, if you care for safety. We will find horses a few steps farther on."

Katherine's doubts were dispelled by the excitement which the peril of capture inspired, and she followed him without any thought beyond that of eluding her pursuers.

As they passed out of the forest she saw a second friar waiting with three horses. She was not permitted time to make any close observation of this new attendant.

Her guide hastily assisted her to mount, and then sprang into the saddle of the second horse with an agility which only one accustomed to the exercise could have displayed. His comrade being already in the saddle, the horses started immediately. As if by pre-arrangement, Katherine's horse was placed between those of the friars, and a leading rein was held by the one who had brought her from the Priory.

This arrangement she did not at first perceive; and even if she had perceived it she would not have been disturbed at the moment. But when they reached the river and their pace was necessarily slackened in order to cross the ford, she became aware that she rode more in the character of a prisoner than of a willing companion.

In mid stream she cast a troubled look backward, and for the first time a serious doubt arose in her mind as to whether the pursuers were friends or foes.

Her guide observed her expression and seemed to divine her thought.

"Your danger is nearly passed, sister," he said, softly; "once we have crossed the river we may defy pursuit."

"But where is Lamington?"

"Safe, safe. Be patient; you will see him soon enough."

" Why do you lead my horse? " she queried again, agitated by the evident irritation of his last response, and that vague memory of its tone returning to her.

" It is a wayward brute, and must be led for your sake. But waste no more time in questioning ; all your doubts will be resolved presently."

She uttered a cry of alarm, for she had recognized the voice at last.

It was that of Sir Robert Cochrane.

As she uttered the cry, she gave the reins a quick jerk, and attempted to turn the horse's head, to recross the stream. But the leading-rein, which Cochrane held firmly, rendered the attempt futile.

Discovering the failure, and without reflecting upon what she was about to do, she made a movement to leap from the saddle into the water. But Cochrane's companion, as if prepared for such a desperate measure, grasped her round the waist, and held her tightly on the seat.

She turned upon the man furiously, and tore the friar's hood from his head, revealing the stern features of her brother.

"Shame upon you, Richard Janfarie," she cried, "to lend yourself to this black scheme. But it shall not serve you. We are followed by those who will give you prompt payment for your falsehood."

She struggled with him violently, screaming with all her strength, in the hope that the pursuers might hear and come to her assistance before her captors were able to start the horses again.

"Be still, madam," said Cochrane, fiercely, at once throwing aside all effort to disguise his voice or to conceal his purpose. "Your cries will avail you as little as your struggles. Those who follow us are our men. I told you that they were pur-

suers only to quicken your pace. It was
no more than another part of the stratagem
which your obstinacy has compelled me to
use to make you sensible of your duty.
Be silent, I say, or we must use means
to still your tongue that I would fain
avoid."

Her heart sank at the revelation of the
device by which she had been betrayed;
but as she heard the shouts of those who
followed, a faint hope presented itself.

He was capable of any deception, and it
might be that he was deceiving her again
in saying that the pursuers were only the
men of Johnstone.

Acting upon that suggestion, she redoubled her efforts to release herself, and
to attract the attention of any who might
be within hearing. But Janfarie held her
fast; and Cochrane urged the horses out of
the water and up the embankment.

Then he halted, and with a cold smile watching the effect which the discovery might produce on her, permitted her to look behind.

The small troop of Borderers had just appeared from the wood, and were galloping down the hill to the river, only ceasing their continuous halloo when they took the ford and saw that their leaders awaited them.

In a few minutes Katherine was surrounded by the Borderers, and she comprehended then with what dexterity her persecutor had arranged his plans; for by the simple means of causing the men to follow he had guarded the retreat, and by the alarm which the idea of pursuit had caused her, she had not been permitted time to reflect upon the manners of her guide or to entertain more than a passing suspicion of his purpose. She had, in fact, become a willing companion in the flight with the man whom of all the world she would have most avoided.

She ceased her struggles now, for she was bitterly satisfied of her helpless position. She would have been hopeless too had not her indignation sustained her.

"You have done brave work, gentlemen," she said, contemptuously; "and you have won great honour in your treacherous triumph over a defenceless woman."

"I regret, madam," answered Cochrane, suavely, "that you have forced us to adopt these measures; but if they offend you, the blame rests with yourself. You will learn by-and-by that in what we have done we have studied your welfare more than our own desires."

"You interpret baseness finely, Sir Robert Cochrane; but you shall not make me accept your reading of it."

"There is the more to be regretted, since you must be guided by it."

She turned to her brother.

"Are you so much this creature's slave that you will not stretch forth your hand to protect me from him?"

"He is your husband," answered Jan-farie, dourly.

"You would have me so," she cried with flashing eyes; "but iterate the claim until your tongues are palsied you shall not find me submit to it. Out upon you both—if you were not conscious of the injustice of your claim, why have you entrapped me thus? Why have you snatched me away from the protection of the Lord Abbot, who pledged himself to test your rights by the judgment of the King himself?"

"That I will answer," broke in Coch-rane, coolly, whilst he adjusted his feathered cap which had been brought to him by one of the men to whom he gave the friar's habit that he had hastily taken off.

"Speak then," said Katherine, viewing him haughtily; "and speak honestly, if you can."

The desperate position in which she was placed, the mental anguish she was enduring, whipped her into a species of frenzy, so that she spoke passionately, and without any regard for the consequences of redoubled watchfulness which would ensue upon her further irritating her persecutors.

"I have removed you from Abbot Panther's care, mistress," said Cochrane, frowning, but still with a degree of politeness, "because he is no fit guardian for one so fair, and because he is too partial a judge of your position."

"He acted as a worthy man should have done; he was merciful to the weak, and he was just to you, who deserved it so little. He offered you fair opportunity to prove your truth."

"You do not know him as I do," was the perfectly cool response. "You are too rash, and in too high a temper to understand these matters now; but I promise you that before long you will be in a better mood. As for the opportunity Panther offered to me, it was one he had no power to deny me, or he would have done so."

"It is your evil nature that sees all hearts black as your own."

"You are wasting words, mistress; but I will give you no reason to complain of my courtesy, and I will satisfy all your inquiries. I have already given you several of my arguments for removing you from the Abbot Panther's patronage. The most important argument of all, however, remains to be told. Powerful as he may have seemed to you in the isolated Priory of Kells, he holds no place of credit in the estimation of their Majesties; and your presentation by him would have been a disgrace to you and to me."

"I am willing to take that risk. If he is in disgrace at court it will be so much to your advantage. Let me return to him, since I accept the risk of what harm his protection may do my cause."

"But I do not accept it, madam; and you must permit me to present you to their Majesties, since I, who suffer most at your hands, have the best reason to cry for justice. I will do so in a manner that even you shall not dare to impugn."

Katherine held her breath; she could scarcely believe that she had heard him aright; for she could not comprehend how he, by whom she had been so wronged, could be willing to place in her hands the

means of obtaining justice from an authority to which even he must submit.

"Will you take me to the Queen?" she
asked; "will you take me without halt or
delay?"

"As fast as horses can carry us," he
said, with the same tone of injured dignity
in which he had last spoken, "we shall
ride to Linlithgow."

"You will permit me to see the Queen
alone?"

"If such is your pleasure—yes."

Janfarie spoke with a degree of relief, as
if his conscience, which had been burdened
by his share in his sister's present predica-
ment, were lightened—

"It was on these conditions," he said,
"that I consented to take part with Cochrane in the trick by which you have been
placed under our control."

"Dare I trust you?" she asked, regard-
ing the men doubtingly.

"You must," retorted Cochrane, "for you have no resource.   But I pledge my credit that you shall be carried to Linlithgow without delay; and you may trust me the more readily when you learn that my own position is involved, and that for my own sake I desire no better issue to the unhappy misunderstanding between us than that which the King may direct."

"Ride on, then," she said, firmly; "since I must trust you so far, I will be no hindrance to your speed."

Cochrane inclined his head coldly, and made a motion with his hand to Janfarie. The latter appeared to understand the motion as a signal, and quietly fell behind, retaining with him four men.

Katherine, surprised, and rendered, if possible, more uncomfortable than before by the retirement of her brother, observed that amongst the four Borderers whom he retained was one of those who had been engaged in the struggle with Lamington at the Dumfries hostelry.

What was their purpose?

She had not far to seek for an answer to that question. Their purpose was to cover the retreat, and probably by foul means to prevent Lamington ever appearing at Linlithgow to uphold his own cause and hers.

Her heart beat quick at the suspicion; but she was calmer now, and she saw that any outburst on her part only served to render her the more helpless in the hands of her callous captor by increasing his watchfulness. Therefore she remained silent, although she sickened at her own fancy of what might happen should Richard Janfarie, burning with desire to avenge his father's fall, and madly attributing that misfortune to her lover, encounter Lamington.

Cochrane, without appearing to observe her anxiety, directed the men to ride close; and then grasping the reins of his own horse and the leading rein of hers tightly in his hand, he urged the animals forward at a rapid canter. He cast no look behind, and he did not seem to give any attention to his companion. His eyes appeared to be fixed on the road straight before him, but all the while with cunning side glances he was noting every change of her countenance.

She rode beside him silent, angry, and yet afraid.

CHAPTER XIV.

IN CHASE.

"Gae, saddle me my coal-black steed,
Gae, saddle me my bonnie grey;
An', warder, sound the rising note,
For we have far to ride to-day."

The Tweeddale Raide.

LAMINGTON was conducted by the Prior to Katherine's dormitory. The door stood wide open, and the chamber was untenanted.

The first thought which occurred to Lamington was that the Abbot had conducted her to some other apartment, and that the Prior had not been made aware of the change. He recalled the latter, who, without having entered the room, was moving away.

The Prior, as soon as he had been made aware of the absence of the lady, hastily went in search of the Abbot. He returned immediately, the prelate accompanying him.

"This was the chamber in which I left her," said the Abbot, looking round him in perplexity and amazement; "and I bade her bar the door that she might not be disturbed."

Inquiries were instantly made, and it was discovered that the Borderers had quitted the precincts of the Priory only a few minutes before; but no information as to Cochrane could be obtained.

On examining the gatekeeper, they learned that Richard Janfarie had departed half an hour before his followers, taking with him two extra horses. Further, one of the men, who had been the last to pass through the gateway, had left a scrap of paper for Bertrand Gordon.

Lamington snatched the paper from the man's hand. It was neatly folded, superscribed in a clear, clerkly style of penmanship, and it was sealed with Cochrane's signet. He tore it open, and read:

"The lady has been wiser to-day than she was yesterday. She acknowledges the proper authority of her husband, and accepts his protection of her own free will, as she was bound to do by the most sacred law. Renounce her: cease your mad persecution of her, if you wish for success in any venture that you make. Do not seek to mar her peace again with your presence if you wish to live.

"ROBERT COCHRANE."

On reading this intimation that all their efforts had been foiled, Lamington knew that Katherine had been trepanned by Cochrane's cunning ; but when he remembered that the Abbot had advised her to bar the door, and so keep out unwelcome intruders, he remembered also that this letter was corroborated by her treatment of him in the morning, and a doubt disturbed him.

But he flung the doubt from him with a furious exclamation.

"No, I will not believe it. I will not doubt her again until I learn from her own lips that she has been deceiving us all. She has been betrayed ; and he would foist this lie upon me, to make me halt in the pursuit."

"Right," muttered the Abbot, who had taken the letter from him and was reading it with frowning countenance ; "right, it is a lie that he would foist upon you. But how has he managed to hoodwink her again?"

"No matter how the trick has been accomplished, we must follow with all the speed horses can make."

"Ay, follow," continued the Abbot, apparently busy with some other thought. "But in what direction?"

"We will discover."

"He has a band of men to guard him, and you are alone."

"I cannot stay to count these hazards. When I reach him, I will consider in what way to outwit him."

"Ay; but stay," muttered the Abbot, reflectively; "there is more in this than the mere question of rescuing the lady —much more than concerns your safety and hers."

"What is your meaning?"

" This. He has got the start of us; he
will reach the King before us, and his
representations being the first made, as he
is the first in the King's favour, will weigh
so heavily against us, that it will require
the strength of giants, and the subtle craft
of the magician, to enable us to steer our
way through this storm that is breaking
over us."

" He will not dare to present such a
cause to his Majesty."

" He will dare anything; it is the very
boldness of his flights which, astounding all
men, and leaving them inactive, have
permitted him to reach the eyrie he now
occupies. You must not judge him by
any common rascal, for whilst you watch
for him creeping stealthily to his purpose
in the dark, he will dash at it—ay, and
attain it—in the broad light of day."

" You have read his character closely,

I can believe; but in what manner will your knowledge of it serve us in the present strait?"

"I fear that it will serve us little; but it will, at least, direct us in the course we should attempt."

"Then that is to pursue the reptile, and strike him down without remorse."

"And be yourself doomed to forfeit life, or to be a hopeless fugitive from the land. We must meet him with his own weapons —courage and cunning; the first, to dare any charge that he may make, and to seize upon it as an instrument to strike him back; the second, to guide the weapon to the vulnerable part of his armour."

"In the saints' name, what part is that?" cried Gordon, impatiently. "Since you will not touch his life, how and where can you harm him?"

"In his disgrace. Once degrade him in

the King's eyes—once assure his Majesty of the real character of his favourite, and Cochrane will fall beneath our feet to be trampled upon and crushed out of memory, as a worthless wretch deserves."

"And if you fail?"

"Then we will pay dearly for our temerity; and, in faith, there is much danger of our losing what little hold we have at present; for if he reach Linlithgow before me, you will find my presence at court forbidden. Give him that triumph, and he will sweep every other obstacle from his path. Albany and Mar themselves may then have reason to dread his power, for their nighness to the throne may readily be made the means of alarming the present wearer of the crown."

"He has not obtained that triumph yet, and swift action on our part may place it for ever beyond his reach."

"We will try it. You follow him, and delay his progress by any means you can find, short of running him through. Take this signet, and if you show it to any of our friends on the route they will give you what assistance you need."

"Who are the friends?" queried Gordon, placing the ring on his finger.

"I will give you a list of them; any one of them will place twenty men at your command at an hour's warning."

The Abbot retired to prepare the list of gentlemen, whose service he knew might be counted upon. Lamington proceeded to the stable to saddle his horse. This task he performed rapidly, for a knight, whose career in those times was fraught with so many surprises and dangers, was bound to accustom himself to every duty that the accidents of war or feudal strife might require of him.

In a few minutes he led the horse out to the court, and was ready to start. He was presently joined by the Abbot, who placed a small tablet in his hand containing more than a dozen names of nobles and barons.

" Master this list as you ride forward," said his lordship, " and then destroy the scroll; for although it would be difficult to make it hurtful to any of our friends in its present form, we cannot calculate what harm it might do them if it fell into the hands of one clever enough to give it the appearance of treason."

" I will have it by rote before I have ridden ten miles."

" That is well; but do not slacken your speed, for Cochrane must be stayed at any hazard."

" And you ?"

" I ride hence on the instant and make

for Linlithgow without halt or pause. Away, and Heaven speed you, for the fortunes of a State may depend on your success or failure."

" If I fail to bar his passage, and to be ready in answer to your summons to appear before the King, reckon me amongst the dead."

The gate was thrown open; the keeper indicated in what direction the Borderers had ridden, and Lamington galloped away from the Priory with heart strung to desperate resolution.

The sun had passed the meridian: the bright tinge which gilds the fields and trees in the morning, had faded, and a dull shade was creeping over grass and leaves. The change was a delicate one, and only perceptible in certain moods; but in that mood the mind becomes keenly sensitive to the dulness which succeeds the glitter of the morning light, when nature assumes an appearance like that of a polished mirror which has been breathed upon. The wind, too, seems to become chiller and to whisper through the woods with more melancholy voice—all with an inexpressible subtlety suggesting the approaching shadows of the night ; and to a mind influenced by circumstances, suggestive of the shades of fortune. There was, besides, a quietude in the atmosphere, disturbed only at intervals by that sad murmur of the wind, the lowing of kine, or the baying of a hound, which oppressed the man with a sense of weakness. He had sufficient of the fanciful in his nature to feel these things, but his present mission was of too high import, and his desire for retribution too strong, to permit them to obtain entire sway over his mind.

He thrust all fancies aside, and setting

himself firmly on his seat galloped forward, skirting the wood, and, led by instinct or by fate, proceeded directly towards the ford of the Ken where those whom he pursued had crossed.

He had covered something more than half the distance between the Priory and the river, when his pace was suddenly checked by the sound of a loud and anxious halloo, proceeding from amongst the trees.

He drew rein, for the voice sounded familiarly in his ears, and presently a large black dog bounded out from the wood towards him, followed immediately by Muckle Will. The hound danced sportively round about the horse's feet, and Will, with long swinging strides, ran up to his master.

The big, simple-looking fellow was very red in the face at this moment; his cheeks were swollen, and he was panting for breath as if he had been running some distance. He rested his hand upon the horse, the while he looked eagerly in his master's face, making signs towards the river and uttering some sounds which were at first unintelligible.

"Take time, Will, take time," said the master, with difficulty controlling his impatience so that his follower might not be farther excited; "take a long breath, and let me know what your grimacing means."

"The leddy, man, the leddy," gasped Will, waving his hand in the direction whence he had come.

Lamington's blood tingled with hope.

"You have seen her," he said quickly.

"Ay, down yonder at the ford," rejoined Will, still panting, but rapidly regaining his breath.

"When—how—with whom?"

Will stared a minute as if trying to fix the questions in his memory, and then :

" Whan—it was just as lang since as it has taken me to run frae the water to here. I was coming to ye at the Priory as ye direckit me last night, but I gaed roun' by the tower to warn the auld folks that ye was coming—— "

" Yes, yes ; but the lady ? "

"Weel, I'm gaun to tell ye—I was comin' doon by Balmaclellan to join ye, when, just as I got near the ford, I heard a woman skirling like a kelpie, and syne, when I got down to the hough, I saw the leddy—your leddy—among a wheen doomed scoundrels, and no a sowl to help her."

" Did you make no attempt ? "

" What could Stark and me do among mair nor a dozen ?   We'd just have gotten our crouns cracked, and ye wouldna have heard a cheep about the business. Na, na; we havena muckle wit, but we have enough to keep whole bones when there's no chance of winning onything by broken anes. So we just got cannily by, and syne ran on to give ye warning."

" What road have they taken ? "

" The straight road through the Glenkens. They'll pass within bow-shot of the tower."

" Hasten on to the Priory, seek the Abbot, and acquaint him with what you have discovered. Then ask him to give you a horse, and follow me."

" Ye dinna mean that ye are gaun on yoursel' to tackle a' thae loons with your ain hand ? "

" I must pursue them. I have means of obtaining help when it is needed."

" Ye're daft. They'll murder ye without speiring whether ye like it or no."

18

"Do as I have told you, and overtake me if you can. They are sure to halt at some stage of their journey."

"Let me gang wi' ye enoo," pleaded the fellow.

"You must have a horse—you cannot keep pace with me on foot."

"I might lift a brute at the first house we came to."

"How, sirrah? Do you propose that to me? Do as I have told you; it will be the quickest way in the end, and your information will be of service to the Abbot."

"Let Stark gang wi' ye onyway; he'll keep ye on the right road after them. They're no riding unco fast, and maybe they'll be taking some by-roads; but Stark will match them."

"Yes, let him go with me, and you come after us without delay."

"I'll be with ye before ye hae gotten

muckle farther than Black Larg"—then addressing himself to the dog and making excited gestures to help his words, he went on : " Here, Stark, take the road and follow the leddy, man. Doon, doon! I'll soon be wi' ye. Be a guid dog and show the maister where the leddy is. Awa' wi' ye."

The hound, as if understanding every word, gave vent to a loud yelp; and with nose bent to the ground, set off at full speed to the ford.

Lamington galloped after his strange guide, and Muckle Will started at a run for the Priory.

The dog led the way across the ford, and up to the mound on which Cochrane had halted to permit Katherine to recognize the Borderers, and to realize the helplessness of her position. Stark paused a moment there, and then with a short yelp continued the route, taking the road through the

Glenkens which Muckle Will had suggested as the one Cochrane and his company had intended to follow.

The dark irregular line of Black Larg raised its giant form high above him, and the grim summits of the lesser mountains —grim in their bareness of vegetation, and with their dark brows of rock—seemed to gather around him as he advanced. At one point of the road his own tower of Lamington lay at only a short distance to the east, nearly at the foot of the Larg, which overshadowed and protected it. But he had no time to give a thought to his ancient home, to which, only a little while ago, he had hoped to lead a bride. It was a desolate enough place for a bride's retreat, but he had thought only of the brightness her presence would make there, and of the strength her love would give him to win back the lands and honour of his family.

But these thoughts were far removed now. He was like·a hunter in full chase, and he had no heed for anything save the quarry.

At the base of the Larg, the road made a sudden and sharp ascent, and a spur of the mountain closed the view of the path he had to follow. Passing round this spur, he suddenly came upon a man in friar's garb, standing in the middle of the way, so motionless that he might have been a figure of stone.

The hound sniffed at him, and with a growl passed on.

Lamington was guiding his horse so that he might pass without injuring the friar, and in acknowledgment of the office of which his hood and gown were the symbols, he inclined his head. The friar abruptly raised his hand, warningly, and seemed desirous of speaking.

The rider halted, for at the movement the idea occurred to him that this man might be able to give him some information about Katherine and her captors.

CHAPTER XV.

THE DRUIDS' CIRCLE.

"The rugged mountain's scanty cloak
  Was dwarfish shrubs of birch and oak,
  With shingles bare, and cliffs between,
  And patches bright of bracken green,
  And heather black that waved so high,
  It held the copse in rivalry."

Scott.

BEFORE it could be brought to a stand, the horse had passed the friar and left him several yards behind. Lamington waited for him to approach, and the man, observing this, advanced slowly, with an appearance of stiffness in his gait.

The moment he had reached the side of the horse the animal swerved from him, but the rider, with a firm hand, checked this eccentricity; at the same time the hound, which had gone on before, came running back and gambolled in front of the horse, barking sharply, and making an occasional run along the road, as if inviting its temporary master to follow.

"Quiet, Stark," said Lamington.

The dog ceased barking and hung its tail, but it began to move round and round the friar, growling as if dissatisfied, until again reproved, when it sat down with its large clear eyes fixed upon the stranger suspiciously.

"You would speak to me, father?" said Gordon respectfully; "and I have a favour to crave from you."

The friar answered in a husky voice, so evidently assumed that nothing save his

impatience to push forward, and the con-
centration of his thoughts on the one
subject, could have prevented Lamington
from observing it. There was even a
gruffness in the friar's manner, as if the
civility with which he spoke was feigned
much against his will.

"I seek nothing for myself, Sir Knight,"
was the slowly-pronounced answer; "but
I have passed a party of men who seemed
to be carrying a gentle lady prisoner.
What harm she may have done I could not
learn, but she looked too young and fair to
be very guilty."

Lamington's pulse bounded with ex-
ultation.

"Good father, you give me the tidings I
am seeking for," he cried eagerly. "In
the saints' name, tell me speedily—how
long is it since you passed them? Speak,
father, I pray you."

" Barely half an hour gone. They had halted in a retired part of the glen, the lady having been taken with sickness."

" Quick, direct me to the place."

" If you will help the lady, I will guide you thither."

" Heaven will bless you for the kindly office. I accept your offer with all the gratitude that a despairing man can give to one who saves him from uttermost agony."

" Follow, then."

" Stay, father; you shall mount and I will walk, for I am swifter of foot than you can be."

" Keep your horse, Sir Knight; you shall have no cause to complain of my pace."

Subdued as his manner was, he made this response with a degree of dogged resolution which prevented Gordon from pressing his courtesy. He, however, dismounted, and walked by the horse's head, the rein thrown across his arm. He was induced thus to place himself on an equality with his guide, first by his respect for the man's apparent profession, and next by his sense of his own inability to control his anxiety without some more muscular action than he could obtain by sitting on the horse whilst it moved at a pace sufficient to keep him abreast with his guide.

Slight as the exercise was, it helped him to maintain a degree of calmness, and to reflect upon the course of conduct he should adopt when he found himself within reach of his enemies.

He was neither so vain-glorious nor so deficient in common sense as to imagine that he, unaided, could possibly cope with a dozen determined men with the slightest prospect of success. He knew that stratagem must be his chief weapon in the contest he was about to wage.

The friar made no comment upon Lamington's respectful arrangement, and taking the opposite side of the horse, strode forward with a rapidity which would scarcely have been expected from him if he had been judged by the gait of his first approach.

The guide presently struck off the road and entered a small glen, through which a burn whimpled with a clear sharp song, and sparkled like crystal as it leapt over the stones lying in its course, worn smooth by its constant flow, or formed into green balls by the moss which clothed them. The fir with its brown cones, the ash, the thorn, and the dwarf oak, flourished in the den, and imparted to it an appearance of luxuriant herbage that contrasted pictur-esquely with the bare-browed mountains which gazed in frowning grandeur down upon it from all sides.

Following the friar, Gordon crossed the burn and advanced toward the head of the glen. As he was still leading the horse, his progress was interfered with by the thick growth of the trees, and the guide consequently outpaced him. The glen was closed in, at the end they were approaching, by a steep hill, over which the burn leapt in a silvery line of spray, forming a minia-ture waterfall and a prism through which the sunlight was reflected in bright colours.

At this point the sides of the glen were also scarplike, and Gordon observed at once that it would be impossible to take his horse by that route to the height above.

He was perplexed for an instant, and gazed eagerly around, fancying that he must be near the end of his journey, and that Cochrane's party was probably lurking somewhere near, concealed from him by the intervening foliage.

The guide paused until his companion had reached his side; then pointing to the steepest part of the hill, which was covered with whins, he spoke:

" We must ascend there."

He began immediately to make his way up through the brush-wood without waiting reply.

" I must leave the horse here, then," said Lamington.

" You can tie it to a branch; it will be safe enough," answered the friar, without looking back.

" Are those I seek near?" queried Gordon, subduing his voice, and of necessity following the suggestion made to secure his horse.

" Very near. You will see them when you have crossed the hill yonder."

Lamington sprang up the brae after him, clearing his way and keeping his footing on the slope with the ease of one accustomed to such feats.

It did not occur to him that the point they were approaching might have been attained by another path, and without the necessity of leaving his horse behind him. Neither did he reflect that should emergency arise it would be almost impossible for him to lead the animal out of the thicket which now enclosed it, without the loss of much time and the expenditure of some trouble. His present object was to reconnoitre, not to attack. He had no reason to doubt the fidelity of his guide, and consequently he could not suspect that he had been purposely conducted in this direction in order to be deprived of the service of the horse, should it become necessary to attempt an escape from unequal foes.

But Stark, the hound, moved by some mysterious instinct, was suspicious of the whole proceeding from the first, and showed by every sign short of speech its anxiety to lead its present master away from the danger on which he was rushing blindfold. His distrust of the friar was marked from the beginning, and several times he caught the edge of Lamington's cloak, attempting to drag him back. But the knight would not attend to these mute signals of peril. He trusted to the man, and he failed to understand the hound, which seemed to be sensible from the moment they quitted the regular road that they were not following the track of the lady, in whose footsteps Stark had been directed by Will to lead the master.

Repeatedly Gordon bade the hound keep down, and the poor brute, submissive to every command, would slink back for a few minutes, and then renew its attempt to attract attention and to alter the course, but only to be again repulsed.

When Lamington quitted the horse and began to climb the steep brae, Stark uttered a low growl that was half a whine, and instantly leapt up to the top of the hill and planted itself in the knight's path, as if to prevent him proceeding farther.

The friar, who had by this time gained the top, darted a quick angry glance at the dog and paused, after moving a few paces from the brow of the den. He watched with apparent eagerness for the appearance of Lamington, and, when the latter rose out of the glen and thrust the dog aside from his path, the friar's lips twitched whilst a smile of satisfaction overspread his features.

At the moment an eagle swooped over

the heads of the men, seemed to stoop toward them, and again rose into space.

The shadow of the broad wings appeared to lower upon Lamington like an omen of coming evil.

But he neither observed the shadow, nor would have heeded it even had he perceived it, so intent was he upon the object of his journey.

The dog embarrassed him by leaping upon him and trying to drag him back, so that he spoke sharply ; and Stark, hanging his tail between his legs, fell behind, but continued to watch the guide.

The friar, as soon as he saw his companion ready to follow him, moved westward into the wildest part of the Glenkens, and appeared so eager to push forward that he gave Lamington no time to ask questions.

The route they traversed was wild and

picturesque; its solitudes were evidently rarely disturbed by human footsteps. Wild-fowl sprang from their nests, the fox scoured across their path, and the eagle, lord of the bird tribe, was startled from his eyry by the intrusion of man. Around them lay the dark dens and the wooded gullies of the Glenkens, with rivulets like threads of silver marking the hill-sides. Above them were the dark peaks of the mountains tipped with the sunlight, but still wearing a sombre brow, and rising like dumb giants keeping watch and ward over the romantic and solitary passes beneath.

"The course is longer than I bargained for," said Gordon, as he stalked beside his silent conductor.

The latter raised his hand, pointing to a narrow pass which they were approaching.

"The end of your journey lies yonder," he answered in a low tone, which seemed to obtain a peculiar significance from the place and the speaker's manner.

The pass was formed by two jutting boulders of rock which seemed to have burst out of the hill-sides, and to have been abruptly arrested in their career toward each other by some sudden freak of nature. The space between them would barely have permitted three men to walk abreast, and the pass might have been kept by one stout man against fifty.

This narrow cleft made a natural portal to a scene of solemn grandeur. The pass opened upon an amphitheatre of hills, which formed the colossal frame of a plain of considerable extent. In the centre of the plain were seven huge boulders of rock, placed at regular intervals, and marking a perfect circle. The stones were so large that it was difficult to imagine how they could have been placed there by human effort—how they could have been carried across the mountains and placed in their respective positions with such mathematical accuracy.

That they could not have been placed thus by any eruption of nature was evident from the character of the foundation, and the fact that they were clearly not linked to the soil in any way. The regularity of their arrangement was also an argument that they had been placed there by artificial means. More marvellous still, a large centre rock was so nicely balanced on a partially rounded base that it could be moved to and fro by the touch of a man's hand, although the united strength of twenty men could not have shifted it from its position. This was known as the "rocking-stone," and several similar stones have been found in the Glenkens, to this day bearing testimony to the strange powers possessed by the ancient Druids.

The seven stones marking the ring was called the Druids' circle; and their grim forms studding the plain combined with the grand silence of the hills to impart an atmosphere of mystery to the place.

Another peculiarity must be noted; outside the Druids' circle, and indicating the cardinal points of the compass, four pits had been dug. A fifth pit had been made within the circle, near the rocking-stone; this one was half full of water when Lamington was led to the place.

The pits were of the kind which have become known as murder-holes, for the reason already explained that they were used by the barons, who had power of pit and gallows, to punish malefactors summarily. The number of these holes spread

over the district, and still visible, suggest
that at one period there **must** have been a
good deal **of prompt** justice or vengeance
executed.

The place was known to Lamington, but
at this moment its weird aspect affected
him with an unaccountable sense of depression, and the total absence **of** any sign of
Cochrane's **party** perplexed him exceedingly. **He** had expected to have been
brought within view of those he sought the
instant he emerged from the pass, and here
was nothing but a solitary space with its
silent guardians looking grimly on.

The friar advanced straight to the rocking-stone and there halted, wheeling round
and facing his companion.

" We are at **the** end of our journey," he
said, morosely.

Lamington looked round hastily to assure
himself again that there were none save

themselves within the range of the Druids'
circle. Then, turning to his guide,
sternly :

" How, sir, you promised to conduct me
to the halting-place of a party of Borderers,
into whose hands an unhappy lady had
been betrayed. If this be a trick to delay
me in my course, it is one for which your
hood will barely save you a whipping."

The friar deliberately removed his hood,
and revealed the person of Richard Janfarie.

Lamington for a second was confounded
by this transformation. The trick, of which
he had been made so readily the dupe,
was plain to him now; and the vain efforts
of Stark to warn him of the deception
recurred to him with bitter regret that he
had been so blind—so obstinately blind—
as to have refused all heed to the warning,
when there might have been time to take
advantage of it.

But regret was of no service, and he roused himself immediately to action.

"By the saints, Janfarie," he cried, angrily, "any other than you would have paid dearly for having duped me in this fashion."

"I am ready to pay the forfeit—readier perhaps than any other might have been," Janfarie responded dourly; "therefore be at ease; your rage shall not lack a butt to strike at."

"I cannot find that butt in you," said Gordon, troubled by his thoughts of Katherine, and of the prolongation of her anguish by his failure to overtake her captors, "and there is no time for words to reprobate your treachery—ay, and your cruelty to one whose happiness you should have been the first to defend."

"My hand shall never be raised to protect a false wife, and the wretch who has made her false."

Gordon's blood tingled and his eyes flashed fiercely, but he checked his rising passion with a mighty effort, and answered calmly, although his lips trembled slightly.

"You are her brother, and therefore you know that you are safe from me; but you shall discover yet how villainously you have belied your sister and me."

"I, safe from you!—then, by my sword, you shall learn speedily that you are not safe from me. You should have stayed your hand in time, if kinship to her had any sanctity in your sight. Fix your eyes on this," he said, pointing to the mourning badge on his arm, "and then you will understand why I have brought you here, and how little your professions of amity will help you against my vengeance for my father's fate."

"You know that I am blameless of his fall—you know that I would have protected him with my own life had I been near when danger threatened him; but your mad rage, and your blind faith in Cochrane, render you as incapable of comprehending my motives as of seeing that you are befooled by a knave."

"You think so," he muttered, sneeringly.

"Some day, when it is too late to save yourself, you will learn that he has betrayed you as he has done all others. But I have no time to reason with you. Farewell; when we meet next I trust that you may know me better."

Lamington made a movement to retrace his steps, but Janfarie sprung forward and planted himself in his path.

"I told you that we had reached the end of our journey here. Only one of us can leave this place alive."

"Stand aside, madman. I cannot draw on you."

Janfarie pointed again to his badge and unsheathed his sword.

At the same time from behind four of the huge Druid stones appeared four Borderers, and Lamington saw that he had fallen into a carefully planned ambuscade.

END OF VOL. I.

PRINTED AT THE CAXTON PRESS, BECCLES.   *S. & H.*

www.ingramcontent.com/pod-product-compliance
Lightning Source LLC
Chambersburg PA
CBHW060555030726
47498CB00005B/1399